It's You, Isn't It?

It's You, Isn't It?

Antony Paschos

Space Wizard Science Fantasy
Raleigh, NC
www.spacewizardsciencefantasy.com

Cover Design by MoorBooks
Editing by Heather Tracy
Book Layout © 2015 BookDesignTemplates.com

It's You, Isn't It?/Antony Paschos.— 1st ed.
ISBN 978-1-960247-44-5

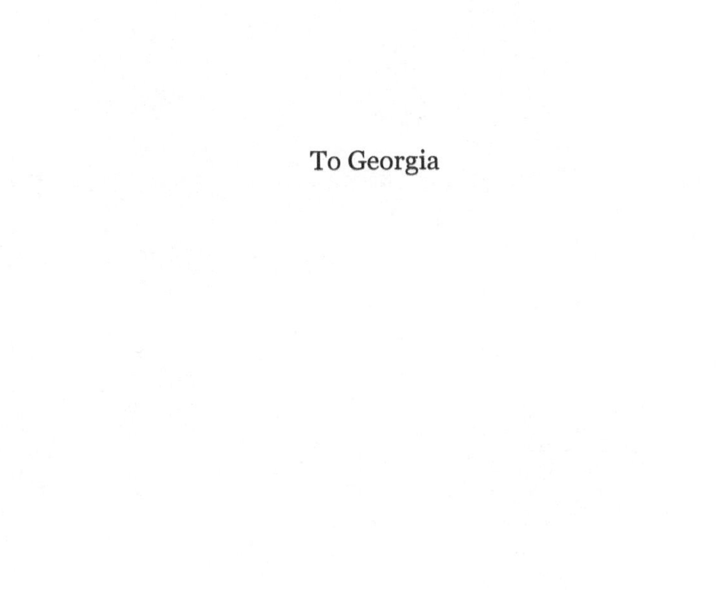

To Georgia

CONTENTS

Present

It's you, isn't it?

These golden-plated fingers bear little resemblance to the coarse aluminum nubs that used to discourage you from touching flowers and leaves and fragile branches. Those stubbles with which you were whisking a healing balm inside a can, the day I left Terra-Octa.

Thirteen una-years ago

The balm you had decocted by yourself, but you let Olia apply it handful by handful on the bark of the young Platanus tree. My younger sister—she was your assistant, your friend, your shadow, wasn't she?

It didn't look alien at all; and if I hadn't been in a local forest and seen how tall and strong those trees could get, it wouldn't look sick to me either. But I knew that it was; there were no veins delineating its trunk, no emerald colorations.

It almost looked like an una breed.

We were in our backyard. You, as always, nurturing the garden. The withered Platanus tree and the rest of the saplings you planted with Olia were here: lemon trees, orange trees, quince trees and fig trees, acacias and a couple of willows.

You, Rocta the Caretaker. The Gardener. Though you were identical to a cheap workbot—plastic façade, silicon lips, aluminum frame and all—you were so much more.

Phaethon—the smaller of the two suns—had already set, but Eleczia was at its descent, painting fiery curves on the skydome cupping New Istanbul. Sitting comfortably under a willow tree's shade, I reached for my lemonade, but my hand froze midair.

The noise geysered through the thrumming of swollen-bellied electric copters skimming back and forth in invisible airways. It swished like a gust—had the town's gel dome given in to external gales? No, there weren't any stray leaves swirling, no rippling of the grass, no ruffling of my hair.

Was I the first to notice the explosion? There, across the slope where our house was perched, in the middle of the comms tower's trunk, blossomed a gray leaf of shattered concrete and rock. The top floor tilted languidly, like a pendulum in its final oscillation. Then it broke off and came crashing down with a whoosh, a mushroom of dust blooming fast across the town.

The hologram of Terra-Una—the Earth—I was watching through my commbox flickered and disappeared. The voice of the history module was cut off. I left the tumbler with my lemonade on the grass and sprang up from my chair. I checked my commbox and stepped away from the willow tree, as if its shade was the reason it had lost its signal. But, of course, it wasn't.

My ears clogged with pressure. I closed my mouth, pinched my nose shut and exhaled in a Valsalva maneuver—plop—why did my eyes water? What was that strange scent? The dirt mushroom on the outskirts of New Istanbul had grown, its hazy mass swelling into the neatly designed labyrinth of buildings like a wave. At the same time, it was soaring towards the crimson sky unbound by any barrier, and yes, the gel membrane insulating the air was truly gone.

I focused on my breath. Three una-years had passed since we had arrived on this planet and studied its XenoMeteorology. If I remembered correctly, the atmospheric pressure outside the dome was slightly lower than Terra-Dua's. Still, there wasn't any shortage of air. There was indeed a strange scent, and did I feel something acrid at the tip of my tongue?

My gaze was drawn to the sight of Olia nestled in your clunky arms, under the withered Platanus sapling. Your eyeholes glared with green light like emeralds and though your plastic façade couldn't express emotion, you jolted your head left and right with apparent alarm. And I had never seen you alarmed.

I was startled. One third scared for Olia, one third jealous of her, one third struggling to keep calm. I was fifteen una-years old, two years older than Olia, and I was supposed to be trained for unpredictable situations—the General's daughters shouldn't panic, should they? I should think, rationalize.

But this was no simulation. The skydome was gone. The air we were breathing was carrying all the local germs and bacteria and there was nothing I could do about it. Luckily, all known infections, however critical, should take more than a day to develop. Yet, the destruction was on the other side of town, far away from our garden and there was no imminent danger. Mr. Stephens, our caretaker, should be inside the house doing push-ups by the hundreds. And Dad's post was not in the demolished comms tower but in the town hall, whose green cupola was—

A louder explosion and a second cloud devoured the town hall's pediments in its gray bowels.

Olia screamed, "Dad!"

My calmness crumbled, my jealousy flinched, then crumbled too, leaving me scared shitless. I darted to your metallic embrace, stumbling on the lemonade tumbler I had left on the grass, and that's when I heard the loudest blast of them all: a bang on our front door.

Sixteen una-years ago

"This is the tallest Platanus tree found as of today." The Xenobotanist pointed a gloved finger at the gargantuan, willow-like Platanus. His constant smirk under his helmet's viewscreen could've been printed, as in a clown-robot's face. "And, let me tell you, kids, personally, I speculate it could be the oldest tree. If the known measuring methods apply to this planet too, then it could've lived ten, maybe fifteen thousand una-years."

Our ship had just arrived on Terra-Octa and everyone was excited, especially me. Though it would take some more years, this would be the planet where I would finally transition.

I just hoped that it could happen sooner.

The Xenobotanist's elation was annoying. After half an hour of him playing tour guide, Olia and I had reconsidered. Maybe Dad's epiphany that even the younglings should familiarize themselves with the new environment wasn't lucky. So, while the rest of the children kept dragging their feet in the Xenobotanist's wake, Penko slipped around the Platanus' trunk. And, of course, Olia and I followed.

The Xenobotanist's babble dwindled to the clamor of the jungle, the creaking of trees, the trilling and the occasional howls of unknown creatures.

Penko was standing close to the Platanus tree. His tight suit delineated his heavy build, as if his body was more muscular than it really was. No wonder he loved wearing it. Unlike me, for the same reason: it emphasized my boyish frame and though it was rather thick, without a skirt, I felt as if my whole crotch was in plain sight.

The tree's trunk was wider than our house being constructed back at the settlement. Long ripples ran alongside its bark, their cavities shaded green, radiating with the vigorousness of an enormous ripped muscle rather than the wrinkles of an old person. Its arteries were a common sight in many trees in the jungle. Most of them looked like crystallized sap tears dripping from their bark, but these were different; these felt alive, swollen, as if they were pulsating imperceptibly, ready to spring the tree into life and tear it from the ground.

If this wasn't a tree but the buried hand of a giant who came to life, I wouldn't be surprised much.

I wouldn't dare to touch it, not at that moment, but Olia ran her gloved fingers along the veins, a playful smile under her helmet's viewscreen. They were phosphorous, their green color pulsing. "I wonder what would happen if we cut one." We could hear each other through our helmet's comms.

"Maybe we should," replied Penko. Though he was twelve, like me, his folly matched my sister's.

I noticed a soldier leaning on a nearby tree, probably avoiding my father's gaze. Even though Dad was appointed General, he took pride in dining, patrolling, even looking after the children along with his troops.

"You shouldn't touch it, Olia," I said.

"I'm the Chosen One," she replied, as if she was even younger. "I'll touch whatever I want."

"Oh, so you're keeping up this fable on this planet too? What's next, imagining that one of those trees is Mom or something?" I couldn't resist the sharp comment.

The fable she'd made up consisted of her being the chosen one and occasionally finding Mom's resurrection in various places. The psychologist had told Dad it was a valid way to cope with Mom's loss, but I doubted it.

"Why not? What if Mom has travelled all the way to here and turned into a tree, waiting for us to come?"

And though her fables bored me to death—or, well, perhaps my sister bored me to death—I must admit she was good at turning "me" into "us," thus dousing the bitterness from my tongue.

Plus, no matter how much I made fun of her fable, she had never called me by deadname; well, neither had Penko. Perhaps that's why the three of us had stuck together.

"Whatever," I mumbled.

Her index finger poked an artery. "It's hot!"

A waft of olive oil passed through my helmet's filter. A constant supply of oxygen wasn't necessary since the air was breathable, but it was supposed to be loaded with bacteria and viruses and who knows what else, right? "Just don't cut it, please."

Penko grinned. "Oh, lemme guess. The *General* told his daughters they're poisonous, didn't he?"

"I—I..."

My sister stepped in to my rescue, and I did feel a bit guilty for the sharpness of my previous comment. "Dad never told us they're poisonous, thickhead. Only *your* dad would say such bullshit."

"Watch it," I said and stopped before I added, "chosen one." I was glad of her retort. Meanwhile the soldier who was leaning on the nearby tree seemed zeroed in on his implant, probably watching a movie or chit-chatting.

Penko plucked an army clasp knife from his pocket. "So, wanna see what runs through those veins or not?"

Olia stretched out her hand. "The Chosen One should do it!"

"Sure," I mumbled, yet to be honest, I was curious about the green liquid that was so rich in Chloron—was it thick or diluted? Did it smell bad? Was it dangerous like the air outside?

Penko passed the knife to Olia, and she touched the Platanus' bark with the blade.

"Hey!" someone screamed. "What do you think you're doing?"

The soldier I'd glanced at before took two strides forward.

Olia flung the knife away.

"Quick!" said Penko and we skipped along giggling. This was supposed to be a one-off trip since our environmental suits were expensive, numbered and the decontamination afterwards time-consuming, so we wouldn't get many chances for a chase in a jungle.

"Come back here!" yelled the soldier.

Penko hurtled himself onto an ivy curtain hanging from the branches of the Platanus and another tree like a tennis net, only a lot higher.

The tendrils were strong and dense like the grasp of a spider's web on the body of a trapped fly. A sweet lemony smell glued to our gloves, sharp enough to pass through our filters, while the slightly lower gravity helped us ape up fast. Soft, furry leaves brushed against our suits and helmets, some flaking off as the entire net shook. We reached the top, scaled down the other side and jumped, me falling on all fours, soil spattering my helmet's viewscreen.

The soldier had been left behind, probably running around the other tree which, though not a Platanus, had a wide trunk too.

"In there!" yelled Penko and slipped under a huge bracken. We crouched under its foliage, its thick shadow obscuring an area larger than our would-be living room. We huddled up, Penko's panting breath counting the ticks of our excitement. I swallowed saliva and let myself lean against his chest, when something rustled behind the plant's stem.

Had the soldier found us? I was frozen, a swelling hard-on chocking inside my panties.

"A... A beetlecat?" asked Penko.

"Could be," I replied.

Or a carrion-mosquito (a vampire, as we'd call them), or a vicious ape-elephant, or perhaps something else—at twelve una-years old I was too young to have memory-modules installed and I had been through the XenoEcology module rather hastily.

Olia took out her commbox and the cone of light illuminated two antennae swaying in the darkness, a body covered in cilia and two rows of insect legs. The thing was the size of a dog.

The cone of light twirled, fell down and turned off. We spurted out screaming in sync.

The light stabbed my eyes outside the bracken. I blinked and halted immediately. Olia bumped on my back, Penko stood beside me. The jungle held her breath, her silence rippling by the murmur of water gurgling from a distant river, dribbling from cupped-shaped leaves, trickling down bark veins and crevices.

"Where are we?" asked Olia.

"Where should we go?" asked Penko.

Something whooshed behind us. The insect scuttled out the bracken, antennae stretched our way, two eyes fixed upon us. No, it was the size of a pony rather than a dog, larger than the infamous centipedes of Terra-Quadra.

"That way!" said Olia and scrammed away. Penko and I kept on her tail, snaking around trees, bushes and ferns. In a small glade Penko's foot got tangled in a vine, faceplanting him on the ground. We crouched near him. His helmet and suit were smeared in dirt but looked unscathed.

"Are you ok?"

"Can you get up?"

I put my hand under his armpit and tried to lift him, but he cried out.

"I—I think I broke my ankle or..."

"Your...your ankle?" stuttered Olia.

"I told you not to run!" I blurted out.

"No, you didn't!"

"Yes, I...well...well, I would've told you if you hadn't run like that!"

"It was Olia who started running!"

"Stop blaming Olia for all your shit!" I replied and she let out a short giggle, for I rarely took her side, or perhaps because I rarely swore.

We managed to get him on his feet, though he was throwing all of his weight on his left leg. Olia swung her head around the glade at every little creak and whoosh.

"We should've made it to the camp by now," I said after we'd stumbled some distance. "I think we took the wrong way."

"Let's turn back. Maybe the monster lost us," said Penko.

"The buzzer!" screamed my sister. "I've lost my commbox. Try yours!"

"Wow, you're right!"

We had forgotten about it. Penko and I took our commboxes out and activated our emergency buzzers, transmitting our position to anyone nearby. We instantly got a ping with the camp's position on the commbox's screen.

"So much for a big sis," said Olia, but she was smiling.

"Shut up."

She didn't quit smiling though, not until we swerved in the opposite direction and came face to face with the centipede.

It rattled two bony-pale mandibles, and I almost lost the ground beneath my feet—if it wasn't for Olia's scream and my big-sister instinct kicking in, I'd have passed out. Still, I lost my grip on Penko and let him sag down with a squeal.

That's when I saw you for the first time. Less than a month since we'd been in Terra-Octa. You stood on an uprooted tree trunk wrapped in a mantle of moss. Shafts of light cascaded through thick foliage straight onto your armor. It gleamed golden, as if it was etched on a Platanus' bark, while the gaps under the thin plates pulsed with emerald light.

"Wha... What is it?" whispered Olia.

I couldn't utter a word. Did I smell a waft of olive oil?

Penko sat on his ass. "Oh, shit..."

Olia elbowed me hard. "Avra!" she hissed.

Somehow Olia ended up in my arms and we hugged each other; it was our first hug on this planet.

Though your armor could belong to a huge, outdated robot, you jumped down with feline fluidity, a faint flute-like whistle wafting as you moved. That's when I noticed flywheels hidden under the pieces of your armor, blurry discs glinting jade in a flawless whirr. What did those cogs move? Was that a pump connecting a junction of veins under your chest-plate? And this green glow, did it come from a hidden web of capillaries branching out all over your body?

"Is she an ape-elephant?" stuttered Olia.

"I don't think so," replied Penko.

"Shut up, both of you!" I tightened my arms around Olia; she was shaking, or maybe it was me, or both of us.

Both of us, yes.

With an almost imperceptible tootle, you approached the centipede—frozen as we were, we had forgotten all about it. Was this blade-tipped rod strapped behind your back a spear?

"I think she's... I think..." muttered Olia, rather to herself than me.

She swallowed hard as you crouched and fondled the creature's bizarre head. I think I heard it purr. Then, it coiled its snake-like body around your legs and disappeared in the shadows of a shrub.

A distant clamor sliced through the jungle's hum, cracking, panting, shouting. With a shrill whistle you vaulted up behind the bushes that swallowed the centipede a moment ago.

Dad appeared, splitting through the briars. His eyes bulged, his composure cracked, and he hugged us in a whirlwind of an embrace, the light shells of our helmets clanging against each other like eggs.

"Ouch!" I said. "You're hurting me, Dad."

He let us go. This was the second time he had hugged us so tight. The first was at Mom's funeral.

"What happened? How did you end up here?" Despite his previous outburst, he didn't crouch to speak to Olia as he still did when he wasn't wearing the uniform. His stature as a General ranked higher than the parenting module's instructions.

We kept silent. The rest of the excursion showed up: soldiers, children, the Xenobotanist,

Penko's mom. Their sighs mingled into one long exhalation of relief.

"Penko Padmanabhan," said Dad as if he noticed him only now that his mom hugged him. "What's your excuse for scratching the helmet I trusted you with?"

Penko opened his mouth but my sister horned in. "I'll tell you everything."

Olia started talking, munching words and entangling the facts. I stood by her, filling in when she needed help. After a while we managed to put the story in line, more or less.

People were staring at each other as we finished up, the Xenobotanist and some soldiers smiling. Not the kids, not Dad whom I couldn't picture smiling while sporting the uniform.

"What's wrong?" asked Olia. "Does this sound like a joke to you?"

Dad raised an eyebrow that razed the soldiers' smiles. He was probably happy about Olia's attitude; though he had lectured us many times on how important staying calm is, he preferred bursts of anger than crying.

Weakness is dangerous. Showing weakness is deadly.

His words.

"Well, the monstrous centipede, sure..." The Xenobotanist coughed in his fist, then turned to Dad. "I mean, General Brahms, we might've not catalogued one, but after all, these jungles do resemble the forests in Terra-Quadra. But... A tall golden robot?"

"Perhaps the excitement of the first time in a protective suit?" said the soldier that had tried to chase us.

Yeah, well, Olia and I had worn various protective suits before, but none was so light, tight and smooth, while the helmets had the largest lens I've ever gazed through; their filters were awesome, their comms transmission was excellent and they were lighter than a jockey.

"Being excited over a suit won't give you hallucinations," said Olia, and I smiled.

The Xenobotanist chuckled. "I mean, an unknown insect, okay, I can accept that. But, come on, a robot on this primitive planet? With armor on? And veins with, what? Chloron?"

Dad gave him a hard stare, which the scientist didn't catch, unluckily for him.

"It was a she," said my sister with the same ferocity she used to correct other kids over my gender.

"Excuse me?" asked the Xenobotanist. "And how do you know that, Miss Brahms?"

I braced myself for another chosen-one rant or even worse, a counter-question like "how does Avra know?" But she just replied, "Well... I just know, okay?"

The Xenobotanist threw me a side glance and grinned. "Well, if it's about imaginary friends, you have the right to choose its sex, don't you?"

The soldiers were looking at Dad, who gave the Xenobotanist another cold stare. Finally, the scientist took notice and cowered immediately; he coughed, mumbled something and filed away with the rest of the crowd. I bet that it was a physical reaction to Dad's posture, notwithstanding his uniform or rank.

Olia's index finger pecked me.

"What?"

"You know…" She gulped down, cupped her hands around her mouth, stuck them to my ear and whispered, "I think it was Mom."

I nudged her away from me. "Oh, stop it, damn it! You're a grown girl; you can't find Mom at every place you go!"

"But… But…"

"No buts. You know damn well she's dead!" All the sympathy I had felt for her wits dissolved in a second; and in my mind she turned back into the little childish little girl that was boring me to death.

"What's wrong, girls?" asked Dad.

"Nothing," I replied.

Olia swallowed a sob.

This was the first time we saw you; and at the same time, the first contact of humans with your kin. And your first action wasn't just welcoming; it was saving us.

But this didn't change much of what the future held for you.

Thirteen una-years ago

It's you, isn't it?

I heard a bang from the other side of the house and thought our front door might have been split open. We stood there in our backyard, Olia and I, frozen in your embrace under the Platanus tree. The long, vigorous lines that rippled along its trunk had grown into withered troughs; its veins had shriveled and stuck unto its bark like the shreds of a long-abandoned spiderweb. The leaves over our heads, once glinting like emeralds, now formed a feeble canopy that would cast a sieve's shadow, too thin to shroud us all. The tree was dying fast, but if we didn't do something ourselves, we wouldn't get a chance to outgrow it, never mind healing it. This opportunity had been wasted a long time ago.

We should leave. We should find a shrub to hide in or perhaps ditch the house entirely—

A scream from inside. Was it Mr. Stephens? I didn't have time to figure it out, as half a dozen chlorobots barged out of the house's back door and stomped on our porch. One looked like a gardener, another was a caretaker and another a butler. The rest were workers in the Chloron extraction business. All of them were wielding human-made rifles and pistols.

As if this wasn't a terrifying sight by itself, the butler pointed his gun's barrel at you and spoke in the strange way most talking chlorobots spoke. His pre-recorded, flat voice chewed the gaps and paused after each short string of words.

"Longest Roots. The humans will never learn. It makes no difference if we're running out of Chloron. They'll harvest us to the roots. You used to have the longest roots of us all. You used to connect us all. Join us. Lead us."

I wondered why he called you Longest Roots and what it meant. Olia had claimed the story you told me the only night you came into my room was true: that the Platani had uploaded their souls into the chlorobots' brains. I had laughed at her, but could she have spoken the truth?

Could you have spoken the truth?

Your silence didn't surprise me. Though you had a speaking module installed too, you'd mostly open your silicon lips to chew dead leaves and frail sprigs—your food.

"Longest Roots. We've been slaves. For three human years now. For how long shall we keep on doing this?" Each sentence the butler pegged like a nail—gesturing with his rifle—sent pulses of shock throughout my body. This felt so unreal, as if I was in a dream.

A dream in which you finally spoke. You dead-panned sentences short and sharp. "Neighbors. For as long as it takes. We decided to wait. And wait we will."

If this was a dream, it was a dream I shared with Olia, cause she started shaking, and you fastened your grip around us, your metallic arms cold to first touch. You smelled of wet leaves and olive oil.

"What... What's going on, Avra?" she whispered. "What are they talking about? Why did Mr. Stephens scream?"

"I...I..." I was the big sister, I was supposed to have the answers, to make decisions. It suddenly dawned on me that it wasn't her shaking, it was me. "I don't know..."

I pinched the skin on my arm, but I didn't wake up.

This wasn't a dream. The butler lowered his gun and took a gray commbox out. Was it smudged with blood? Chloron from the bots' plasma? He fiddled for a couple of seconds, then turned a holo on.

A coldness pierced through me like a sharp blade. It was Dad, sporting his suit and tie. He was with the prime minister, the governor, the consul, a scientist and a few congress members in the town hall, discussing their plans about Terra-Octa: more people coming in, more bots, more logging machinery. They were speculating why the Platani trees and the plants richest in Chloron wouldn't flourish on other Terras. Dad suggested trying a couple of newly found planets whose soil might prove suitable and the scientist introduced terraforming solutions that should offer a more hospitable environment for them. Some politicians from the opposing party, the Pacifists, were raising rather mild concerns.

It was a secret recording and an old one too. Penko, who was into hacking whatever was supposed to be secret, had shown it to us almost three una-years ago.

"Longest Roots. This is what they'll do." The butler pointed at us with his rifle. "These children. They're the seeds of destruction. Let us reap them. Now."

Your story that the Platani had uploaded themselves in the chloropunks didn't seem so stupid now.

Damn. Olia must have been right.

Your grip tightened, as if your arms were tethered to a screw that wrenched in, squeezing me against Olia's body. The earthly scent of the ointment she was applying before swirled into my nostrils.

"Neighbors. These children. Can be the seeds of change," you replied. "These children. Can become our future gardeners."

Your answer to our guests made them look at each other. Your words were comforting, yet locked inside your constricting hug, I couldn't help but think if we were your prisoners.

Olia brought her lips close to my ear—her breath smelled of orange juice. "You... You think Dad's..."

"Stop it. Please. He's fine."

"Yeah, but what about Mr. Stephens?"

"Shh."

As the ping pong of prerecorded bursts kept on, the cardiogram-shaped outline of the buildings of New Istanbul crowning the horizon had turned into a fertile field for destruction. Plumes of scree spurted out, flourishing into smoke cauliflowers. Another huge building (was it a mill or a warehouse?) was demolished and a missile hit a copter, bringing it crashing down. Through the rattle of gunfire—faraway and nearby, reminding me of the huge sawing machines—fizzed loud screams. Could it be Penko, from his house next door? Or his mom?

Your arms were now smothering us, your stump of a finger wedging my ribs apart as you spoke.

"Rocta, stop it, you're hurting us," I grumbled.

My sister let out a small cry. I tried to nudge myself out of your cage of arms but it was steel strong.

"Longest Roots," I tried instead. "Please…"

You didn't back down an inch. My neck touched your shoulder and the freezing aluminum burned my skin. Were you going to hand us in?

Then, Olia said: "Stop it… Please… Mom."

She used to call you "Mom" in front of Mr. Stephens to remind him that though he was our caretaker, he would never replace Mom. But she'd rarely do so in front of others.

I cringed, but your grip loosened a tad.

Then, a clang came from inside the house. The unmistakably controlled scutter of soldiers' footsteps and from a corner of the building a shadow moved. Voices screamed too loud to be contained in the intercoms, "The chloropunk's got the general's daughters!" The lightning of gunfire flashed out of the corner of the building, from a window, from everywhere inside the house. Bullets pierced and glanced off the crude human-made exoskeletons of the chlorobots whose heads turned to the sources of the havoc; too late to locate the soldiers who had probably already taken positions.

They were too slow to react. Two went down, the rest scooted off for cover in the nearby trees—pointless, really.

"Mom!" screamed Olia at my ear.

Instead of releasing us, you picked us up and ran. We were small of frame, yet I didn't know your cheap bot skeleton possessed such strength or you, such decisiveness.

You skirted around the trees in an awkward, wobbly run, and it dawned on me that I had never seen you run in this body. The shots and the screams from behind us wouldn't cease ("the bot's kidnapping the general's daughters!"), a branch snagged my shirt and another whipped me—it smelled of lemon.

But now a howl of a human indicated that we weren't alone; the chlorobots were returning fire and keeping the soldiers at bay for the moment.

In front of the garden's backdoor, you put us down.

I touched my cheek—hot blood, no, it was just a scrape. Only then did I notice that a herd of pink clouds had gathered on the horizon.

Olia didn't waste time; she thumbed on the pad of the electronic lock and the door opened with a click. You heaved us both up again and burst out on the streets.

The relief of you saving us gave way to the realization that despite the low gravity, you were slow, as if you had spent all your energy to get us out of the house. Which wasn't true; like all chlorobots, you were in a cheap bot body with a speed limit that was lower than an average human. But, up until now, I was too numb from panic to see it.

"Rocta, let us down!" I yelled. "We can run."

I thought you wouldn't do it. I still wasn't sure if you wanted to save us or hand us in to another group of chlorobots. But you halted, crouched and let us down gently. We were outside Penko's fence, still in our neighborhood.

I leaned on the wall to catch my breath, all this while I was suffocating. Perhaps we should flee from you but what would we do alone? Where would we...

"Avra!" Penko's voice.

I turned and recognized his gait, limping slightly since what he initially thought of as a sprain in the jungle three una-years ago—back when we'd just arrived in Terra-Octa—proved to be a crushed ankle. He halted beside a green Chloron-coated dumpster. His shoulders were shaking, a shoe was missing, a sock drenched in mud—blood?

Olia darted to him. I screamed her name and immediately regretted it. I just wanted to get to him first. I caught up with her and we crushed into him and hugged him. I'd never seen Penko shed a tear, but now a hot runnel wet my arm and we couldn't stop him from shaking.

"What happened, Penko?" asked my sister.

I wanted to scold her. He was in no condition to answer any questions.

"My-my-my..."

"We must go, Penko," I said but he kept stuttering.

"Olia..." I said but he spoke.

"Mom's dead... Dad too... Killed them... They killed them both..."

"Who did?" I caught myself asking without thinking—I already knew.

Four chlorobots sporting worker's outfits showed up outside Penko's house. They raised their guns.

Penko shook us away with panicked jolts. "They did..."

Fifteen una-years and six una-months ago

War is a pest that humans lug with them. Even if we don't get to start it, it gets to bug its way into everything we touch. I don't need my memory enhancement module to recall Dad's sayings. The most accurate ones were those he'd only voiced once.

It was dong-winter, half an una-year after the first time I saw you—and I had almost ended up believing the people who said you were just a fairy tale we three had made up; a clockwork killer-elf zoomed out of proportion by our childhood imaginations.

Not Olia though. "Think we'll see Mom again?" she asked.

"Oh, gimme a break..."

We had gotten sick of various craftsmen fiddling in our house. After so many months, they still struggled to fix what they had installed hastily in the first place. So, we were now sitting together with Penko on an uprooted tree trunk outside the establishment's walls.

Olia sighed, looking at the truncated forest around us. Hundreds of stubs protruding from the ground.

"And don't you dare mention her in front of anybody," I added. "Unless you want them to stare at us like we've gone nuts or something."

"You know, having people believing you're a little crazy, isn't so bad as it sounds..."

I almost snapped that she knew all too well how it is to have people believing you're nuts. But, luckily, before the words slipped out of my lips, the truth of my answer struck me like the cold shower I took a few hours ago—yeah, the boiler was inoperative again. And, suddenly, I saw Olia for what she was: a girl with an imagination that nobody took seriously. Not even me.

I reached out and rubbed her back. "Well," I said, "didn't the Xenoecologist claim that we're not the first to arrive in this planet?"

"Yeah, but when I asked her if..." said Penko.

But I didn't let him finish the sentence. "I know, I remember her reply."

She had replied that there were no traces of living creatures from another planet.

"But I also remember Olia's reply." Olia and I shared a compromising smile. She had said, "Have you checked the mirror?" and the whole classroom that consisted of kids from different ages, since this was a seminar, had laughed.

Penko cackled. "No wonder she asked to do the seminars into each separate class after that!"

I felt a bit dizzy, as always whenever I had to wake at the start of the second twenty-five-hour cycle of the fifty-hour local day. Dad used to say that the human biorhythm was always twenty-five hours, and Olia used this information to claim that we were extra-terrestrial even on Earth. And though the light was artificial in the spaceship that had brought us here, I was still finding it hard to sleep in the middle of the day and function at half-light for the rest of its duration.

I turned my stare in the distance. Phaethon was setting after Eleczia, lengthening the evening and brushing the skydome above us with glinting vermillion bows. It was a beautiful sight, as if the suns wanted to reward us for waking up to see it. Out of the dome, the machines of the logging site at the jungle's outskirts were glinting green, coated with solar panels made of Chloron.

Olia got up. "I'd like to see Mom again though."

I sighed. She wouldn't let this go easily.

"Oh, come on Olia, you don't even know it's a she," said Penko. "I mean... Who the hell knows what they are?"

"I know it."

"How?" Penko replied.

"Cause..."

"Oh, please, Sis, spare us from your chosen-one-know-it-all nonsense this time", I snapped.

Olia frowned. I felt a bit guilty. I could hear a whole dialogue with Dad in my head:

You didn't protect her against Penko.

But it's just a conversation.

Still, you could take her side.

But—

No, buts, Avra, you're the oldest sister and it was two against one.

This dialogue would always end with me in silence, swallowing the fact that he always took Olia's side in those arguments; it was always the big sister's fault.

She put a song in her commbox, took a fat branch for a violin and pretended to play along. Her voice was hardly heard in the crashing of chopped trees, the droning of electric copters and the buzzing of massive electric motors driving the skidders, the knucklebooms, the swing yarders, the woodchippers and the rest of the logging machinery that had just arrived from Terra-Dua together with more civilians and cheap workbots.

The Chloron fever was on since its discovery a couple of una-years before we came—the extraction of the element running in the Platani arteries and, in lower quantities, in the rest of the local flora. It was light, solid and elastic, like plastic with steel's strength, as Dad had said. It was suitable for a million applications from weaponry to musical instruments, like the guitar Dad had bought for Olia which, luckily, she had stopped playing after a couple of weeks. But it was best for solar panels and gel membranes for skydomes like the one that arched over our heads, fencing a yard outside the establishment's walls—a yard that might extend up to a few hundred meters away at the moment, but it was expanding by the day.

The song finished and Olia tossed her branch-violin away.

"By the way, I wasn't gonna say that I know it's a she just because I'm the Chosen One."

I sighed. Convincing her that she's not the chosen one was a losing battle; a battle I'd rather let Penko fight alone.

"Then?" he asked.

Olia put the commbox back in her pocket. "Well, she didn't have a willy dangling between her legs, did she?"

I cut Penko's laughter with a harsh, "So?"

"I mean…"

"You meant what? And what about me? I *have* a willy. Does that mean that I'm a boy too?" I wasn't being fair to her; she always took my side, but I just couldn't help myself, and no memory of Dad's lectures would keep my anger at bay. I was too bored, too confined and too dizzy on this new planet, and I had to lash at someone.

"What I think Olia meant," said Penko, "is that if that robot-thing doesn't have a willy, then the highest probability is that it's a she."

"Oh, thanks for the clarification, Penko, thank you very much." I felt my cheeks burning hot and I hoped I hadn't blushed. Not in front of Penko. He always acted cool around me, but damn me if I had the slightest clue that it actually meant something. Why couldn't I fully transition just a bit earlier? I shoved my hand in my pocket, wrapped my fingers around my blocker tablets. *Breathe.*

"Maybe these things don't have sexes," he offered. "Or they might have different sexes, who…"

The screams from the logging site interrupted him. Some motors idled, others got louder as a couple of trucks sped away from the jungle's brink. Behind them scurried a cohort of workers and a bit further away, their workbots struggled to keep on their toes—in vain, even the most sophisticated models were electronically hindered from outrunning an average human.

"What are they running from?" asked Olia.

Penko got up. "There, see that—ouch!" He sat down on the hollow trunk and caught his ankle.

Six una-months now and three operations and his broken bones hadn't healed properly, and at the age of twelve, he was too young for prosthetics. Guess I wasn't the only one eager to grow up.

"What?"

"There was a shine," said Penko, rubbing his ankle. "Over there at the logging site, in the distance. Something was shining so bright."

"It was a skidder, you fool, I saw it too." To be honest, I hadn't seen it; I just wanted to get back at him for rooting for Olia before.

I regretted my words as he sighed, putting his hurt foot on the ground. "No, it wasn't," he said. "It was in front of the skidder."

He took out his commbox and turned on the binocular app. Olia too. I puffed dramatically, mumbled "kids" but followed suit. On my screen I saw workers running; all of them, as far as I could turn the commbox's view. Some had lost their helmets. They were outside the skydome which meant that they had breathed the air. It wasn't lethal, but they'd need medical assistance sooner or later.

But this didn't seem to bother them at all. Their pace was desperate, panicked.

Penko was right, they weren't running away from a skidder. Under the shade of green harvesters, feller bunchers and woodchippers, an array of strange creatures had gathered.

I reset my commbox's view, unable to believe what I saw, and at the corner of my eye, I realized that Olia and Penko were doing exactly the same. To no avail. What I had seen was true.

On the small screen, the human vehicles looked like toys, and the creatures would have reminded me of some kind of mechanical insects, cast out of a young adult adventure episode, with their spears and swords and glinting armor, that is, if half an una-year ago, I hadn't seen you. And there you stood among them, taller than all of them, prouder, ferocious. I had only glimpsed you for a few seconds, and though I was too young to have a memory enhancement module installed, I was certain it was you, their leader.

Olia mumbled a word, and I think it was "Mom," and though most of the time I used to cringe at her whenever she brought up her mom-fantasies, this time I felt a tiny pang of hope. Sure, you weren't our lost mother, but you had saved us, right?

I filled my lungs with the air, and it was cool, earthly-scented and sweet. Childish as it may sound, hope turned into vindication. All those people fleeing, did they believe in golden robots now? My pride was short-lived as I zoomed into the dark stains on the automata's spears and swords. Then I noticed the dead bodies of guards and workers. Butchered, mutilated, gutted, torn apart. Sprawled legs, arms, heads. A couple of strange animals were sauntering around—carrion-mosquitoes, pink and fleshy. One had already sunk its proboscis into a soldier's corpse and fed.

I screamed.

Thirteen una-years ago

It's you, isn't it?

You spoke in your robotic voice, only quieter. Then you patted my shoulder and whispered, "Avra. I'm talking. To you."

"Okay," I whispered.

"Avra, I said, 'When I charge, start running.'"

"When... Wait... What?"

With one move you tugged the dumpster in front of us, then shoved against it and started wheeling it towards the chlorobots. Once again, I was taken aback by your strength that should've been limited like your speed. Or, perhaps, it was the light Chloron-made dumpster—an extravagance of the early days.

"Avra, Olia." Your voice, flat yet loud. "Run now."

We took off. At the same time, a blast shook the earth and Penko lost his balance, but Olia and I seized him and helped him on his feet. A sepia cloud was building up fast around the corner and Olia hesitated.

"Move it!" I screamed.

I shut parched lips and my teeth crunched powdery dust. It had a faint acrid aftertaste. As we scrambled around the corner, I glanced back and saw you throwing the dumpster at the chlorobots and running our direction. You were slow, but thanks to the guy who once upon a time had decided to limit the speed of the workbots, our hunters weren't any faster. I had never heard of robots turning against humans in any history module, but now, on a different planet, after so much time, the insightful decision could save lives.

Our lives, for one. We caught Penko by the armpits and lugged him, coughing from the dust and the effort. Though I got tired soon, I strived to keep up with Olia. I should've known better than VRing the shit out of my spare time. I guess all the gardening Olia did was now paying off.

Perhaps my younger loony sister was wiser than I thought.

"Enough," I finally cried and almost dropped Penko.

She didn't laugh at me. She was trying to catch her breath too. Dust was slowly dissipating, revealing cotton clouds clustering fast in the sky, hiding the firmament and Eleczia, which would set last. You caught up with us and glanced around with jerky moves, as Olia wrapped her arms around your waist.

"Don't leave us," she was mumbling. "Don't leave us alone, ever again."

Dark spinach-colored stains wetted your overalls. The chlorobots hadn't chased us but they had shot you.

"Rocta... Are you okay?"

You steadied your gaze on the street to our left. I saw another band of chlorobots advancing our way. It wouldn't take long for them to notice us.

"There!" Penko pointed at a dark alley just behind us. We hid in the heavy shade of two buildings, Olia, Penko and I, still panting.

He took out his commbox.

"Spare the effort, they don't work," I said and then, "Rocta, what's going on here?"

You kept silent.

Thunder crackled. Storms in Terra-Octa lasted for hours, maybe days. My mind was finally racing, trying to put the pieces of the puzzle together. Was this convenient for the rioting chlorobots? What would Dad say? Maybe it was, though they probably hadn't anticipated it, since weather forecasting was inaccurate at the moment—something about the satellite constellation that I'd missed on the XenoMet module.

Met module—shit, what had happened to Mr. Stephens? He'd screamed, hadn't he? True, Olia and I never liked him, especially now he and Dad had considered marrying for an una-decade. But that didn't mean we wanted him dead.

The band of chlorobots passed in front of us. Their frames were dented and smudged which didn't seem strange, but some carried rifles, others handguns, one rested a flamethrower's tube on its shoulder.

And at their sight, finally, the pieces of the puzzle clicked together. We had destroyed their forests. We had plucked them out of their proud, ancient armor and forced them into those cheap robotic frames. And, from some sort of Guardians of the Forests, we had enslaved them to workers and servants.

And if what you had told me that night—what Olia actually claimed was true—that the Platani had uploaded themselves in the chloropunks before they came to us, then this was even worse.

Perhaps, all of this was a plan of the Platani.

I wanted to ask you about it, but one of the chlorobots said something and the rest of the team halted.

We were right behind them, and I could see through their array of bodies that steered towards the street across from the alley. They had spotted a family—mom, dad and two kids—scuttling around a curbed building.

Olia jolted and I tried to cup her lips with my palm, but she nudged me away.

"They'll hear us," I hissed.

"Shit, look," whispered Penko.

Luckily for us, the chlorobots were busy aiming. The parents realized it was too late for all of them to escape. They exchanged some words—each offering to sacrifice, I guess. That moment of hesitation was enough. In a barrage of gunfire four bodies flailed. Three collapsed on the pavement. The boy dropped on his knees. A couple more shots and he slumped down too.

The chlorobots moved on, their thudding footsteps sinking in a swamp of explosions, gunfire, screaming. The words of a Pacifist speaking in the parliament rang in my mind: *The General forces the people to pay for way too many weapons, way too many explosives and way too many soldiers for such a primitive planet.*

"We must go," I said.

"Where?" asked Olia and I felt the pride of the big sister press down on my chest. She was counting on me, and I had to work out a way to save us. But where should we go?

"Avra. Olia. Penko. To the spacedrome." The voice belonged to you.

Fifteen una-years ago

When I installed my memory enhancement module, I spent a week binge-watching my past life on replay, and was surprised from my memories' details. That early qiu-summer morning that I saw you for the third time, an una-year since the first, I must've watched a hundred times.

Penko suddenly logged out of the VR mass-multiplayer—we were a killing duet—after merely half an hour of game time. A couple of minutes later he burst into my room. As he took a moment to find his breath, I couldn't help but notice a sparse stubble outlining his chin. I ran a finger on my cheek, tracing the reassuring softness of my skin.

"The chloropunks!" he said, still panting.

I flung back my VR chair, its wheels reeling clean on the floor—all details in our house were finished and the furniture was new. "What about them?"

From Olia's room we could hear her desperate trills with a Chloron-made flute Dad had given her as a gift. Its sound was like a dissonant whistle.

"The chloropunks!" Penko said again. "They... They..."

Penko meant your kin, of course. At first, everybody called you automata. Then, some tried to pass the term "Guardians of the Forest." The word chlorobots prevailed but didn't take long to degrade to chloropunks, especially among the soldier ranks and boys like Penko.

"Oh, come on, Penko, one vid was enough, thank you."

I meant the forbidden footage of chloropunk ambushes that supposedly were increasing alarmingly the last few una-months, to the delight of Penko who was spending hours on the web in search of every possible conspiracy. After he'd found the first video of Dad talking in the parliament, he had hacked the AI of our house—it was easy since it was newly installed as well—and managed to force it into helping him. Olia didn't have a problem at all with him sneaking into Dad's files, and as for me, well, after nagging a little bit, curiosity won over maturity. Perhaps the fact that my heart was beating faster at his presence played a part too.

Anyway, in his favorite vids, the chlorobots would appear out of nowhere at logging sites, slaughtering people at will. They wielded their weapons with silent ferocity, their flute-whistling moves in tandem with the brief crescendos of their victims' screams. They never left a single member of their own behind—at least, that's what Penko claimed—so no one knew much about them.

"It's no vid, Avra, they're outside the walls! Get dressed and let's go!"

Olia had ceased playing or it was Penko's words that sank the room into silence.

"Outside the walls? You mean... They penetrated the skydome?"

Passing through the skydome was like passing through a cascade. Its gel membrane permeated with little force, moistening your suit and reforming as soon as you got past it. Yet for some reason the automata had shunned away from it, like most local animals did. No one really cared to find out why; at least to my knowledge. I guess we all had taken for granted that we're safe while inside.

Quite a surprise to find out that we're not, right?

"Yeah, they did! We're under a fucking siege, right now!"

"A siege? Wait, weren't you the one saying that they don't stand a chance against us in open war?"

"I was! But your dad— Wait, you know nothing of his latest tactics?"

"Which tactics?"

"Well, haven't you noticed the black clouds?"

"I...I thought they were coming from the Chloron mill..."

Penko cleared his throat. "No. Look, your dad equipped the guards with flamethrowers, right? So, at each ambush, the soldiers retaliated, and they kept flaring their way up into the jungle. They fuckin' reduced entire areas into ashes."

"I...I had no idea..."

"Anyway, it worked. The chloropunks must've been pissed off so bad, that they fuckin' left their holes. There are more than we ever thought. There are fucking thousands of them!"

"Oh."

"Yeah. Now, get yourself up and let's go, we're gonna miss the show!"

"What show—"

"Just get yourself ready!"

"All right," I mumbled.

If it was my sister, I'd definitely scold her. We had all seen what the chlorobots were capable of. Yet Penko asking me to join him in one of his dumb schemes almost felt like a tryst and I couldn't help but slip on some clothes as fast as I could.

I was putting on my shoes when Olia barged in too. She had ceased playing the stupid flute, luckily, but she was all dressed up. Before I had a chance to protest, she said, "Look, I had a dream yesterday, okay?"

"Of course, you had." I pushed her aside and went down the stairs mumbling, "Again." Whenever something happened, she'd dreamt of something.

"It was Mom, all right?"

I would've replied that, of course it was Mom, but I felt a pinch of pity for her, which was the reaction I'd get during the first weeks she had started the Mom bullshit; and the flashback to these weeks brought back all the weariness and boredom that smothered me as she was repeatedly reminding me of Mom, as if she was the only one entitled to her memory.

And now I was angry, so I opened my mouth and...

"Where's the little gang going?" Mr. Stephens—our nanny as Olia called him despite his bodybuilder's body—took a sip from a jug of a white glop. It was a protein smoothie with greenberries, a local fruit—his best recipe, very nutritious, very disgusting.

At his dissonant baritone voice struggling to sound happy, I exchanged glances with Olia, my anger dissipating fast. We'd never waste an opportunity to irk each other, but against Mr. Stephens, we were a team.

"Why did you turn the TV off?" retorted Olia.

Olia was right. The holo was off, quite strange for him not to watch his favorite gymfeed post workout, as if every day would bring up some new type of exercises that would pump up his already bloated muscles.

Mr. Stephens claimed to have been drafted for the marines, but Dad supposedly hindered his application in order not to lose his child-nurturing skills. Despite his deltoids that protruded like upturned pears as he shrugged, I highly doubted that. "No…" His voice started out deep and he coughed and corrected it to a slightly higher pitch; the childspeak, as Penko had explained to me and Olia, after reading one of his nanny manuals. "No particular reason."

The fact that he had ripped off these manuals maybe explained why his attitude felt so fake, or perhaps it was because Olia and I had to find a scapegoat to funnel all of our anger, unless we were going to kill each other.

In this strange kind of way, Mr. Stephens' presence did help us. "Now, do you mind informing where are you going?"

"My place," replied Penko. "Mom's had a day off and baked biscuits. Told me to invite the girls too."

Mr. Stephens narrowed his eyes. "You sure, Penko Padmanabhan? Because I'm calling your mom later, all right?"

"Sure," said Penko and went for the door, looking unconcerned.

I got out last and shut the door, silencing Mr. Stephens' wishes to have fun.

Once outside, I scanned the horizon for any of the black clouds that Penko mentioned earlier. There were none. Only the curves of the skydome's gel umbrella glinted under the rays of Eleczia.

The sky was also empty of copters. A silence loomed, amplifying all sounds—a brief conversation, a far-away drone of a vehicle, a knock, a rustle, our footsteps as we rolled downhill.

"What are you gonna do when Mr. Hulk calls your mom?" asked Olia, untouched by the strained stillness.

Penko was striding fast, limping slightly—his ankle probably wouldn't fully heal until he had prosthetics installed. "Oh, he won't dare." Plump as he might be, when it came to foolish ploys, he mustered unfathomed amounts of vigor.

My sister wouldn't back off. "Why?"

He didn't reply and I caught myself smiling. I knew why, and Penko knew why, and, come to think of it, Olia knew why too, she had just asked without taking her time to think.

We arrived at New Istanbul's walls. They were built recently with Chloron-infused solar tiles that supplied a hefty percentage of the town's electricity. It was Dad's idea; a compromise with the Pacifists who kept asking for more solar panels, while at the same time he seemed to have predicted we would eventually need some sort of fortification.

These kinds of decisions were probably the reason he had made a name for himself as an insightful General.

A few soldiers buzzed in the wall's roots but most of them were stationed on the parapets. Penko ushered us around unattended camo tents to a small staircase on the main wall.

"Hey!"

My sweat-soaked t-shirt suddenly felt chilly.

A young soldier stood outside a tent. "Aren't you the General's daughters?"

"Yeah, and we... We..."

He approached and grabbed Penko's arm. "You come with me, rat."

With Penko in his clasp, Olia and I couldn't help but follow him up to the fortifications, where more soldiers crammed the rampart.

Crouched behind mortars and canons, their stillness was fractured by slight movements: switching positions, cracking limbs, clasping and unclasping their fingers around the grips of their guns, wiping sweat from their foreheads despite the regulated temperature inside the skydome.

A lone figure stood behind their rows, straight poised, arms crossed, head protruding from the top of the battlements, alone in its familiar defiance or negligence. If Dad noticed us, he didn't show it.

The soldier came close to him, saluted. "Sir. Your daughters. Sir."

Dad's eyes were hidden behind sunglasses. His scoldings, laconic as they were, comprised of the words that stung the most, to the point we'd probably prefer a beating. Yet Dad stuck piously to the parenting module's instructions, and he'd never punished us—despite Mr. Stephens' repeated empty threats that we had grown to ignore.

I had to tighten my leg muscles to stop from shaking. Worse than any of our childish ploys would've been to show weakness in front of his army. We were the General's daughters, and I was fully aware of that.

Nervous whispers were welling up in the looming silence.

"What the fuck are they doing?" asked a sniper with a huge rifle. Was he talking about us?

"Attacking, I guess?" someone hissed back. Oh, okay, no.

"Attack? With those cleaves?"

"They look more like spears to be honest..."

A distinct cough from my father cut the conversation short, and I could only guess that Olia and I had passed Dad's test of showing how calm we were—as for Penko, he was so used to being caught in all kinds of shams, he had trained his poker face to perfection.

I stole glances at the soldiers. They straightened their barrels and gazed through their sights, frozen in tense stillness. I lowered my head. Black rubber streaks smudged the green-tinted tiles—the soldiers' boots probably.

Dad would harangue us later for sure, but for now he was probably satisfied with our display of solemnity. "So, I guess you came to see the automata." Dad wouldn't call them anything else.

"Yes, sir," I replied. Was he deliberating between driving us away and making a lesson out of the situation? Or would he turn the situation into a demonstration of parental boldness? I didn't think so. The last time we made a fool of ourselves publicly was on that excursion in the jungle, and he hadn't shamed us.

Truth be told, he had never shamed us in front of other people.

"And, Penko Padmanabhan, are your parents aware of this visit?"

Penko gulped. "No-no..." This wasn't Mr. Stephens threatening to call his mom. "Not yet." This was the General. "Sir."

Dad snorted. "Okay. I appreciate that it was you three who first reported one of the automata, to everyone's scoffing. But coming up here is not a game."

I let out a sigh of relief.

"Yes, Dad, but the Platani spoke to me last night..." Olia couldn't keep her mouth shut, couldn't she. "I mean, in my sleep. They said that they're just protecting their forest. Their home. They weren't lying, were they?"

The Platani are not protecting anything, dammit, their guardians are, I thought, but I kept it to myself.

"This is not the right place to talk, Olia." Dad nodded to the soldier standing behind us. "Get my daughters and their friend to a safe place." He turned to us. "We'll have a talk later." Of course, we would.

He turned to Penko. "With you too, Penko Padmanabhan."

"Yes, sir."

"General," the soldier said. "Just one word, if you allow me, sir."

"Go ahead, Private."

"Congratulations on predicting this attack. What will the Pacifists say about our army's presence now, huh?"

Dad nodded and the soldier gestured.

I noticed flashes in the soldier's eye—was he messaging his superiors of the General's new assignment or was he complaining to a friend about us? Whatever he did, he grabbed our hands and pulled us. I tried to steal a glimpse through the rampart, but I could only see the morning sky through the gel dome.

"The dream argument was a great idea," I said to Olia.

"At least I tried," she replied.

"Of course you did."

A few meters away the soldier halted. He was a young lad and his breath smelled of that alien mint that thrived in the jungles, the same one Penko was getting addicted to lately.

"Okay, since you came here"—he threw glances left and right—"I'll take you somewhere where you can see everything, all right?"

Penko's eyes bulged out. "Really?"

"Yeah, well, you know, you'll get a scolding later on anyway, right? And, by the way, I was young too, once."

My sister tried to reply with something but I nudged her—we had to run to keep up with him as he trotted down the stairs. He opened an iron door and led us through dark corridors.

"So, Penko, why won't Mr. Stephens call your mom?" whispered Olia as we scaled up a stairway.

"Oh, give him a break and stop being such a bug, Olia!" I said and she shut up. I knew the answer. Penko's dad had caught Mr. Stephens flirting with his mom—Mr. Stephens was bi, just like our dad.

The soldier led us into a plain room. "There," he said, but we had already huddled up by the largest window.

Rows of automata cluttered the flattened area outside the walls that Dad had ordered built, their long spears pointed to the sky. Soot smutted their golden armor, boots of mud had clotted on their legs and their joints were black with grime.

"Oh my god, there's so many..." mumbled the soldier.

Their helmets were studded with emerald dots that shone through their eyeholes like flashlights. This should have been something new, though without a mem-mod I couldn't be sure.

"You think they're aliens?" I asked the soldiers.

"The chloropunks? Well, they didn't come with us, did they?"

"No, I meant..." I meant to ask if they're from a different planet too, but then Olia horned in.

"You think they'll attack?"

"No idea," he said. "But they don't stand a chance. Not with those spears of theirs."

"Then, why did they come?" asked Olia. "Why now?"

The soldier shrugged.

I caught Penko staring at me.

"The flamethrowers," I said.

Eleczia had soared up high and Phaethon was slowly rising too. The air inside the skydome was breezy, yet the earth outside its gel umbrella should sizzle. Then, with the fluting of a thousand joints in tandem—as if a band of pipers trilled the same feeble note—the automata threw all their weapons to their feet, raising a clamor of thuds that sent us tumbling. My palms joined Olia's and Penko's in a trembling clasp.

"What... What was that?" asked Olia.

The soldier replied first so I missed the opportunity to scorn Olia ("Hadn't the Platani told you in your dreams?") which was good; every time my fear donned the guise of anger directed at her I felt like shit later on.

I tightened my grip, smothering her palm, but she didn't let go of me.

"I think they're surrendering, Miss Avra."

"I'm Olia," she said. This wasn't rare. It seemed as if the whole colony confused our names despite me being taller.

"Olia, yeah, right, sorry 'bout that."

"It worked," mumbled Penko. "The flamethrowers worked. They realized they can't win this war."

The soldier grinned. "I'd like to see what those fucking Pacifists will have to say about your father's tactics now."

This didn't come out of nowhere. Though I wasn't deep into politics, I'd chanced upon holo newsfeeds where the Pacifists—the opposing party in Terra-Dua—condemned Dad for pretty much anything: the very walls that were protecting us, the army's size, even his own presence in Terra-Octa. What I used to find strange was they had people supporting them in here as well.

"But why isn't anyone moving?" asked Olia.

"Well..." said the soldier. "Guess they're waiting for us to do something?"

"And why aren't we doing something?" Olia kept firing questions at him.

I finally let go of her hand. "Because this could be a trap, Sis. And Dad is not stupid."

She frowned but didn't quit. "What kind of trap? They just gave up their weapons."

"Got a better idea?" And, well, I couldn't resist anymore. "Maybe the Platani told you something we don't know?"

Olia zipped it—a medal in my older-sister-performance which would make me feel like shit later.

"Oh, damn," said the soldier. "We're opening the gate..."

A lone figure looking the size of an ant against the army of automata trod on the razed land, soldiering on toward them.

"Look, Avra! It's Dad!"

"Of course, it's Dad," I replied though I wished he wasn't. "He's the captain, isn't he?"

"Well, it's actually *General* Brahms but..." munched the soldier. A furrow cut deep through his cheek—his jaw was clamped, perhaps withholding a comment about Dad's boldness or temerity. It wasn't just the fact he walked straight to the enemy. The detergents in the air supposedly expunged the bacteria that were carried in when someone passed through the skydome, but this was a whole army he was marching to.

Still, his gait was lax, his arms waving slightly as if a display of confidence outweighed military formality. He stood in front of the enemy ranks, inches away from stepping on a spear with his boot. His proximity to them made me even more nervous, as if he invaded their personal space, forcing them to change their minds, or triggering a trap.

A giant automaton took a step forward, trampling the spear in front of it.

"It's Mom!" said Olia.

This would've unleashed a burst of anger from me, if I wasn't frozen.

"Don't worry about your dad," said the soldier who must've misheard. "Our snipers got his back, no chloropunk can harm him." His Adam's apple springing up though, suggested otherwise.

"I said *Mom*," said Olia.

"Who?" asked the soldier.

"Never mind my sister's imaginary friends," I said, desperate to end the conversation and take in all the details of the moment.

Olia muttered something unintelligible and took out her commbox. I turned the binoculars app in mine too with a pang of jealousy. I should've thought to first, at Dad's appearance.

And this was the third time I saw you. Dad raised his head to look at your helmet—tarnished, dented, smudged. Two viridian dots scintillated through your eye-slits.

My heart was thudding so hard I thought the rest would notice.

Dad saluted you and waited. A dark pool of sweat stained his back as if the skydome's temperature regulation was broken. A moment of utter silence stretched long enough to choke someone holding his breath—I gasped. I started counting. At twenty-six, you stepped back from the fallen spear. Dad stooped.

He picked it up—and did your eye-slits flash? He held it with both hands and turned his back on you. You could probably crush him with a single jab.

The spear was long and looked heavy, yet Dad raised its blade high for everyone to see. A star glistened at its edge, in the crossing rays of Eleczia and Phaethon that were refracted imperceptibly by the skydome. A rumble shook the fortress as the soldiers cheered in response.

I didn't share their excitement. This could still be a trap. Dad turned to you again, spear raised. He stretched his hand, stepped forward and merely managed to touch your helmet with its blade—if you were a few inches taller, your head would be out of his reach.

How much time had passed since I heard someone breathe in the room? I didn't know as I didn't know why or how you comprehended Dad's act.

You knelt to him, and we all exhaled simultaneously; and only then did I realize that our hands had reached for each other again.

With a thousand whistling notes, the rest of the automata followed suit. A tide of soldiers gushed down the walls to surge through the gate and join Dad outside. We watched them in silence as they collected the kneeling automata's weapons. As if adhering to a strict plan—which was probably true since they were all communicating through their implants—a couple of huge trucks parked outside and the soldiers started piling the gleaming weapons on their truck beds. I was still afraid something was going to happen. This could still be a trap. Maybe another army of automata would crop up at the jungle's outskirts, or the ones that surrendered would suddenly pick up their weapons. *And if they attack, they'll kill Dad.*

Luckily, nothing happened.

"Ok, kids..." The soldier pointed a finger to his eyes—small flashes indicated he'd just received new messages. "New orders. I have to get you to your house."

I exchanged a glance with Penko. He shrugged and we let the soldier lead us outside. He put us in a small vehicle and drove us up the hill of our neighborhood.

Perhaps it was the narrow cabin, forcing Olia's body to smother me against the vehicle's hard, plastic door. Or the coldness of the window glass on my cheek or the humming of the electric motor. Or it could be something completely different, yet at the passing waves of people crowding the streets of New Istanbul (smiling, hugging, laughing, dancing) I felt so distant, as if I was watching their celebrations in a commbox's screen, on another planet, at another time.

I let my mind fly outside the walls that hemmed in the humans' joy, over the automata who were still getting stripped of their weapons. Laden with dirt, grime and soot, they had kneeled to save their forest from our flames.

Thirteen una-years ago

It's you, isn't it?

You herded us along the streets of New Istanbul to the sidewalk of Brahms Avenue—named in honor of Dad—through smoke so thick it hid the domeless sky. A flash of lightning brightened up the sepia soup every now and then, churning and frizzy and turbulent, only to become foggy again until the next bolt.

With a yelp, Olia sagged to the ground but you caught her. You gently craned her head as she threw up.

"Are you okay?" I asked her after Penko and I coughed our lungs out.

She nodded.

After she finished retching, you eased her down. I noticed a trail of spinach green splotches marking your track. Your plasma had mottled Olia's tee too and the stains looked thick. Did it clot? Its constitution should be similar to the plasma running through the local trees, but I couldn't recall if the Xenoecology module mentioned anything about it clotting.

Were you going to die?

"I'm okay," said Olia, coughing a little bit more.

You moved towards the dust cloud again.

"Where are we going?" she asked. "The subway's in the opposite direction..."

"Rocta's right, Sis. There's no need to take the subway." I pointed at the sky. The launching of starship lifters interfered with the skydome's integrity, so the spacedrome was outside of it. But now the gel was gone, so we could just walk there.

"Then at least, can we keep out of the dust? Please, Mom?"

I resisted the urge to jump on her. I was sick of inhaling dirt too.

"Yeah, we can try that way." Penko pointed at a side street.

The buildings at its flanks were chewed up by an explosion, their bare bricks looking like broken ribs. A crate obstructed its entrance with a crown of piled up concrete chunks, while a couple of crumpled cars were strewn around— Wait, was that a corpse lying beside it? No, it was moving slightly.

Silent, you took another step towards the dirt cloud.

"C'mon, Mom, please?"

"Olia! I said Rocta's right," I almost yelled. "She's taking us through the fog so we won't be seen."

"Yeah, Avra, but that street looks deserted too," insisted Penko.

The body—a woman—moved and out of nowhere a carrion-mosquito, large as a cat, landed and flapped its ruby-red wings.

"Look, Avra, a vampire," whispered Olia.

The mosquito sauntered towards the wounded woman who was sifting a blind hand inside the detritus. An acute whiff of Olia's puke suddenly made me nauseous. A shot and the mosquito jolted, its swollen belly exploding in a short-lived flower of inky spatter. The woman tried to cringe—a second shot blasted her to stillness.

I couldn't help myself. I puked greenberry jam and orange. Olia gave me a napkin when I finished, and Penko offered those chewing gums he loved so much. The alien mint washed away the putrid tang of vomit.

We finally moved on. A whirring pealed at each of your steps. You were hurt and probably running out of plasma.

Raindrops started to pour down—a strange sight in those streets since the meteorologists scheduled the rains inside the dome mostly at night, in order to not reduce the panels' efficiency. The rain grew stronger; it soaked my hair and rinsed my face of mud. I lapped the soily moisture to soothe my sandpaper-dry mouth and sore throat.

This brief relief kicked in a train of thoughts. How did the chlorobots manage to wreak so much havoc? I mean, I knew Dad had hoarded a lot of weapons and explosives anyway... But, why now? What had changed?

You stumbled on a soldier's corpse. You picked up his rifle and a couple of mags. Did I know him? He was lying face down and I'd have to turn his head to see his face—and I wouldn't do that. We sped up our pace and soon we were soaked. Though the rainfall made the dirt fog ebb out faster, it grew so heavy it blurred our vision. The clap of thunder, the shots, the explosions and the occasional screams dwindled into white noise, and I gave in to an acute feeling of calm focus—had I grown numb or was it the air that got cleaner?

"Where are we?" said Olia, panting.

"Just keep walking," I replied, a bit too sharp. "Sis," I added to soften it. Dad said that we should stick together in a crisis, and if this wasn't a crisis, I didn't know what it was.

What had happened to Dad?

Despite the dust settling down, it was hard to orient amidst hollow walls, piles of debris, crates and careened vehicles. We passed by a crashed copter. The four propellers at its corners had been warped like spaghetti and the glasses of its windshield and windows were shattered. There was no sign of a pilot, but it could just as well have been flying while remote controlled—a rare situation and only in easy routes.

"Look there, across the street," said Penko. "It's the town hall."

Olia yelped but my heart sank. Behind the faint brush-streaks of dissipating smoke, the neoclassical buildings of the town hall were reduced to heaps of stone. Gone were the shiny pediments and only a couple of stumped columns stood upright, like half-cut trees in a logging site.

Like the Platani that were harvested regularly.

The place was strewn with dead soldiers, and I slowed down. I braced myself; I had to see if Dad was among them.

"Someone..." said Olia but stopped abruptly.

"What?"

I thought I heard your arm creak as you squeezed her palm in yours. Rain was splashing on your frame and a rivulet was sliding under your other forearm to your rifle, spilling drops of water and plasma from its barrel tip.

"Nothing," muttered Olia. "I just thought I heard someone speaking."

I tried to listen; the occasional thunder, the crackling of guns now and then...was that a cry? If it was, it was distant. No talking though.

"I thought someone called our names," said Olia and stifled a sob.

"Well, not anymore," I replied.

"We need to move," said Penko.

You steered her across the street, me and Penko stringing along. A gray floury blanket shrouded the concrete chunks that once were the town hall's walls, gnarled steel bars jutting out of them. The dregs of dust caking the ruins rose to a cloud as we huddled up in a nook and I stifled the urge to cough again. At least we were safe from the rain. Our hearts attuned in a common, thundering beat and though my soaked clothes were getting colder, I was feeling hot inside.

Had they lost us? Maybe they never spotted us.

A distant thunder and one of us jolted, scaring the rest—I don't know, perhaps it was me. In its wake, the small sounds picked up again— the murmur of rain, the crack of detritus settling down, a rustle, three long panic-laden exhalations. Coppery puddles were swelling in the muddy streets, welling up in the craters and holes.

"Where's Dad?" asked Olia.

I took a small walk, checking the closest dead bodies. I didn't even have to upturn any of the bodies lying face down. Dad wasn't among them.

Then came back to the place where you stood—a niche among the rubble of the town hall's walls.

The stares of Olia and Penko were pinned on my lips, tense with anticipation, and I couldn't help but remember the first time Penko had kissed me, not long ago. We had been studying mathematics in my room.

"Well, he's not here."

They exhaled in unison.

Through the flimsy shreds of fog emerged four silhouettes. Treading carefully, sporting camo pants, holding rifles.

Soldiers. One of them gestured, another one nodded like in the movies of the previous century, when the marines didn't communicate through implant interface in robot-like coordination. Now, they stood still.

"Dad?" whispered Olia.

"Shh," I said.

They wouldn't hurt us, right? I should spring up, tell them we're General Brahms' daughters. Surely they'd help us. But what if they didn't recognize us? The destruction had affected comms, so without their implants' functions they might be more prone to shoot us.

"They're soldiers," yelled Penko and sprang out of our niche, always quick to react.

Olia squealed, you got on your feet, I cowered behind your legs. The piles of destroyed walls wouldn't protect us from the bullets if we got into a fight. We had to be careful.

But Penko had a different opinion.

"Hey! In here!" he yelled.

His cry drew the soldier's barrels. "There," said someone.

They were pointing our way.

"This was the voice I heard before," said Olia.

"This isn't Dad." The moment I uttered the words, I felt stupid. Of course this wasn't Dad.

Everything happened faster than the lightning that struck close to the town hall. One of the soldiers opened fire, the deafening crackle, the tinging of bullets ricocheting off your frame, Penko's scream, your cold barrel rubbing my shoulder as you raised your rifle and shot back.

Fourteen una-years ago

Penko and I were alone in my room, studying mathematics. We were sitting next to each other on my bed. Like yesterday and the day before, my nostrils had clogged with the smell of this alien mint, as Penko kept flinging gum after gum into his mouth. I had only one and hoped my breath didn't stink. The blockers were a blessing, sure, but, for me, they weren't enough. And I wasn't allowed to continue with my transition procedures for another three una-years, so I was reluctant to try out anything with anyone. Sixteen had never felt so far away.

Penko was struggling to clear up an equation but our mouths' proximity made it harder for me to grasp the meaning of it.

I smiled. "I don't understand shit."

I could swear all I wanted without Olia around. She was confined in her bedroom since the time she claimed that she'd left the skydome's protection and taken a walk in the jungle—which had led to a half-month detention in the hospital until she admitted her lie.

Penko's face lit up. He had just torn a chewing gum's cover. The chartreuse paper was illustrated with a Platanus tree sketch. He held it but didn't bring it to his mouth. His stomach growled in the silence. Or was it mine?

"What's wrong?" I asked.

He crumpled paper and gum into a lump, tried to tuck it in his pocket but ended up dropping it on the mattress. His eyes closed and his lips twitched as if he muttered something. Then he opened his eyes again.

"Can... Can you understand this, then?" He spelled the words like he recited a poem.

"Understand what?"

"Thi-this!"

Later, I understood that he had rehearsed this speech and was referring to his try at a first kiss but as he lunged his head, he ended up bunting me like a charging buck.

I flinched and rubbed my nose.

"Oh, wow..."

But Penko wasn't one to give up. He tried again and this time he managed to kiss me without inflicting any damage. His lips were dry and rough, and his tongue was probing for a way inside my mouth, and though it felt slimy and warm, it brought me an immediate arousal in the form of an uncomfortable hardon.

Neither the kiss nor the hardon were meant to last for long.

Three knocks on my door.

"You know the rules, Miss Brahms," said Mr. Stephens' muffled voice.

The rules were no closed doors in the company of strangers.

"Damn," whispered Penko, a dreamy grimace on his face.

I gulped down—was my saliva a bit thicker or was it my impression? It certainly felt that way, as if Penko's mixture had thickened it. And could he hear my heartbeat, or did it just shake *me* to the core? Shit, it was probably my imagination making things...taking every little detail and amplifying it to extremes. I guess in a way I wasn't too different from Olia.

"Yeah... Damn."

Penko checked his commbox. "Oh shit, I gotta go."

He bounced off the bed. I wanted to tell him to wait a second, but I was too numb from his kiss too.

"We can repeat this lesson another time?"

"Sure," I said, feeling as if I was talking to myself. He had already squeezed through the doorway, and I rushed in his wake.

Downstairs, Mr. Stephens had the holo gymfeed on while cooking—his post-workout meal probably. Though he had a chef's diploma and was an apt cook, Olia and I would never admit it openly. In fact, we did our best to refuse to eat his food for the slightest reason—too cold, too hot, too whatever. But despite our attempts, it was almost impossible to make him angry. I suppose that the parenting modules had prepared him for such childish behaviors.

I got past Penko and opened the front door for him.

He tossed a "Good day, Mr. Stephens," and left.

I sat there, watching him. The grass carpet in our front yard glistened. The meteorologists had scheduled nightly rains for the whole week inside the sky-dome. He took a few rearward steps on the wet pavement, staring at me as he walked away. I smiled, but then he stumbled and faced forward again.

I laughed, shut the door and went to the kitchen.

"Nice polish," said Mr. Stephens without turning to look at me.

I had painted my nails a Terra-Dua night sky blue, dotted with stars. This wasn't the first time but it was rare. Most of the times I was bored, and even when I wasn't, I did it in a rush.

So, he had noticed. And if Mr. Stephens had noticed, Olia would notice too.

I shrugged, opened the fridge and grabbed a chocolate drink and a protein bar. I hadn't had breakfast yet and Penko's kiss had whetted my appetite.

"So, did you and Mr. Padmanabhan study?"

"Yeah, I guess."

"Good, because we have to complete the math test today. Remember?"

He had recently caught Olia using Penko's hacks so he was present in all our tests—offering me a good excuse to scold her in the absence of other reasons. "I know."

Olia came downstairs, went straight for the fridge and got some protein cookies Mr. Stephens had made yesterday.

Her eyes bulged at the sight of my nails. She opened her mouth but I gave her a scowling look and nodded at Mr. Stephens. I didn't expect her to understand that I didn't want us to fight in front of him, but she did. She smiled cunningly and winked.

She munched a cookie. "Is it true that they stripped the chlorobots from their armors?"

Mr. Stephens smiled in earnest. "Where did you hear that, Miss Brahms?"

"Trees told me." She went to the sink and spat dramatically. "Those cookies are charred." She took an orange juice from the fridge.

"Oh. I'm sorry 'bout that. Maybe it was just the one you had now, 'cause you ate half the baking pan I cooked yesterday."

"I was hungry," said Olia. "So, why do that? Why strip them?"

"Don't you think they're dangerous in those huge, armored suits, honey?" Somewhere in the slides of a wannabe stepparent's module must lie a recommendation to answer questions with a question.

"No," replied Olia. "Trees told me that they're servants and mean no harm."

I smiled, chewing on the bar. Lately, I was bored of my sister's mischief even when she was directing it at Mr. Stephens. But after Penko's kiss, I thought they were fun. I chugged down the chocolate drink.

"Well, I guess if the trees told you so, you should definitely tell your father, cause it was his suggestion to the congress."

Olia didn't fall for the Dad-trap. "They'd be more useful in their own armor."

"Perhaps. But what if they try to revolt? Oh, wait, the trees told you they wouldn't, right?" He smiled a robotic smile. "Listen. It's no secret our resources are limited and the more resources we ask from Terra-Dua, the higher the commission they'll leech out of us will be. So, putting them in workbot frames was an excellent idea."

He was getting into details to discourage us from further questions. It was a technique Olia and I knew well because I'd used it excessively myself against her.

"You think Mom is with them too?" asked Olia.

Mr. Stephens frowned. "Who do you mean by 'Mom'?"

"No one," said my sister. "Never mind."

He took a deep breath and clasped his hand into a fist. If the veins on his arms looked like swollen rivers, their estuaries were ready to burst on the back of his hand. I bet he cursed us silently. He opened his hand, stretched his fingers and talked slowly. "I'm sure your mom is somewhere watching you girls. But I don't think that place is on this planet."

His tranquility was outrageous, but I kept thinking of Penko's kiss.

The front door clicked open, sparing him from the conversation.

Under our doorframe you stood beside Dad. The hood of a black shirt concealing your metallic skull barely reached up to his broad shoulders. You had tucked your aluminum hands inside your pockets and if it wasn't for the whiteness of the plastic façade attached to the front of your skull, I would've mistaken you for a short human.

"Welcome, General Brahms," said Mr. Stephens. "And who would your companion be?"

Dad came in and you followed with the slightly clumsy gait of a workbot. "Well, someone had to set an example for the rest of the people..."

Mr. Stephens smiled. "It's a great idea, General Brahms. I was just explaining it to your lovely daughters. And what's the gentleman's name?"

Dad glanced at you. You could be just another cheap model if it wasn't for those emerald dots gleaming through your eyeholes. "Actually, it's a she. Right, Olia?"

I was going to complain to Dad—I didn't need another person in our house—human or robot—but Olia scrambled across the living room with a screech and—*clunk*—she slammed into you and wrapped her arms around your waist. I let her put on her show and didn't interrupt her.

Mr. Stephens brought his hands on his hips. "Olia Brahms, may I ask where that expression of joy is due? Is that chlorobot a friend of yours?"

"Well, she's the automaton that gave her spear to me that day..." said Dad.

"Oh, yeah. And such a bold move. Totally you, General Brahms."

I had kissed Penko, all right, but Mr. Stephens' tries at flirting with Dad were now getting on my nerves.

Olia narrowed her eyes. I knew that look of pure venom very well and though I was older I wouldn't want her directing it to me. And I was glad, since I thought I knew to whom she'd target it. "Oh, Dad..."

"Yes, honey?"

"Is it true the memory enhancement module doesn't let adults forget about their lost loves?"

Dad's Adam apple sprang up. He could probably see in which direction she was steering the conversation too. "It is."

"So..."

"But you can choose to keep certain memories away."

Olia's face lit up. "Oh! So you don't mind if I call her 'Mom,' do you?"

I felt a pang of anger—Olia was asking Dad to suppress memories of Mom in order to play her stupid Mom-game to hassle Mr. Stephens.

"No, honey, I don't," said Dad.

"So, she was the leader of those...chlorobots, wasn't she?" asked Mr. Stephens.

"Mommy, Mommy," chanted Olia.

"She was," said Dad. "And I decided to name her Rocta. You know... Since she's like the first indigenous robot in Terra-Octa..."

But Mr. Stephens had prepared a comment for his previous question. "Keep your friends close and your enemies closer, right?"

The sly bastard knew Dad loved hearing people reciting his sayings. Mr. Stephens hid his mouth with his palm, a T of veins bloating on his swelling bicep under his short-sleeved tee—a gesture I bet he'd practiced in front of his mirror. "Mmm, maybe I should become your enemy then, General Brahms."

I wanted to throw up.

"Mommy," repeated Olia. "I knew you'd come, I knew it!"

And Olia didn't help me either.

Thirteen una-years ago

It's you, isn't it?

I remember how deadly your kin can be, and I realized how the chlorobots wreaked so much havoc, when you shot back right after the soldiers fired at Penko.

Human restrictions on your workbot body may hinder your speed, your stamina and your strength. The creators of the bots hadn't thought about accuracy though; or they had, but they just couldn't afford workers who weren't precise.

Anyway. All it took was four shots and all four of our enemies were dead. They never stood a chance against you.

Olia sprang out of our nook, and I admired her courage. I wished my knees didn't shake, my frozen feet hadn't turned into wood inside my shoes, and I didn't have to think of every step until I inched to Penko's body. His gaze beamed upwards, to the clouds above, uninterrupted by blinking, and his eyes bulged out as if they were made of glass. I slumped down so close to his lips, remembering the first time I had kissed them, and then the other times, when we had managed to stay alone without Olia or Mr. Stephens.

Holding my breath, I listened for Penko's heartbeat, as we've seen in movies together.

Olia placed her ear on his chest and we both lingered for any sign of life: a heartbeat, a twitch. I felt your fingers on my hair days later, your iron caress, hefting the finality of Penko's death, tethering a burning knot around my throat. I raised my head, hot lava welling up in my eyes. Olia choked back a sob. I couldn't make a sound.

I blamed myself for that moment, but I blamed you too. Would Penko have lived if I had spoken out? Would those soldiers have opened fire if you hadn't been with us? I guessed I'd die with the regret of hesitation.

I tried to lift Penko's body; I had felt it on mine, naked, in the past and I could've never imagined that it could weigh so much. I turned to you, tears on my cheeks. Your own body wasn't in good shape either; your clothes stained with thick dark plasma.

I knew that there was no use carrying him, yet I tried.

"Please?"

You shook your head in denial. Olia's palm rested on my shoulder, electrifying me but I resisted the first urge to throw it away. I let myself fall into her arms and cried.

Had I cried before in her embrace? I don't think so.

"We have to go," said Olia after a while.

"Where?"

We both turned to you.

"To the spaceport," you replied.

"Oh." I felt so empty, I couldn't think if this was a good idea.

"Yeah, weren't we heading to the spaceport already, Sis?" asked Olia.

"I guess."

She hugged me tighter, then finally let me go.

We carried on in a blur, Olia and I, dimly aware of our surroundings, limp by fatigue and hopelessness. And you, hobbling your creaking aluminum limbs with iron will. You left a trail of dark splashes behind us. We plunged our shoes in crates and grenade holes full of mud, we stumbled on lumps of swollen tarmac, deep cracks on the pavement, parts of broken vehicles and corpses. Somehow, you managed to steer us clear of chlorobot teams and I watched with a sense of detachment as you shot down more soldiers.

We clambered up the heaps of detritus that just yesterday fenced New Istanbul, then crossed the warehouse district outside—they were built recently and following your surrender, there was no need for fortifications. The road through the plantations and the greenhouses was flooded. My feet were frozen and my drenched shoes weighed a ton as we sloshed about ankles deep in water. The cold must've woken me up cause when we finally got to the spacedrome hub, clarity had returned.

The arched rods supporting the building's photovoltaic cupola jutted out above us like the ribs of a gargantuan monster. The vault had been shattered into large sheets of fragmented glass that creaked under our wet soles. The solar panels blanketed what was once the hub's concourse and we had to cross a jade landscape of splintered plains, dented hills and shallow pools that looked like molds for giant glass fish, the smithereens stamping their scales. We trod on strewn aluminum bars, which once formed the ceiling's lattice construct, now bent and askew like threshed wheat. We snaked around poles sprouting in clusters of iron birches, stepped over crashed down luminaires that spread their pieces like flowers, passed a toppled x-ray cage that reminded me of an upturned Platanus tree and the stumped trunks of lone pillars that looked like freshly logged trees. Below the fractured, malachite meadows lay rows of chairs, counters, tables. A dead security officer stared at me below the glass like a drowned man under an icy lake.

My knees bent on their own and if it wasn't for Olia, I would've crashed on the floor.

"Oh fuck," she said, "he looks just like..."

Penko, yes.

I held my tears, but the rain wasn't so merciful; it kept washing over me. "Yes. But we need to go."

A hot wind picked up, whipping our faces with raindrops. Gunfire rattled non-stop and seemed to emerge from two areas—the first one somewhere close and the second further ahead, outside the demolished hub and stifled by the roaring of huge turboprop engines.

So, this was no wind. The lifter was about to leave its bay. We reached the other end of the hub, sheltered behind a fence of short concrete barricades and took a peek at what was left of the apron ahead of us.

The lifter to the starship in orbit looked like a huge white spider. Eight curved legs craned out from its main hull like the skeleton of an umbrella, its turboprop engines fixed at their barbs hovering it ten meters above ground level. A scattered crowd of frenzied people struggled to cross the destroyed apron, racing towards the lifter's loading ramp that was still connected to its bay. Every now and then, someone stumbled over a chunk of asphalt, fell in a ditch or was shot down by enemy or friendly fire; a group of chlorobots had settled behind the ruins of a wall on our left—this should have been the first area of concentrated gunfire. Some got up and sought cover behind toppled vehicles, others shuffled on only to collapse again—they were probably picked up as easy targets.

Straight ahead, behind a bulwark made of debris and two wagons of a careened truck, a team of soldiers defended the lifter's bay, shooting back at the chlorobots.

"Dad," said Olia. "Dad is there, Mom. We need to go there."

You paused. The plasma had spread all over your clothes, a constant whirring echoed inside your frame and even the slightest move you made came along with a flutter. How serious were your injuries? I had no idea. I sneezed. My clothes and shoes were frozen and the rain wouldn't cease. I was starting to feel numb inside; I wanted all this to end like a bad dream. I wanted Penko to be alive and waiting for me, with his foolish jokes and smell of alien mint.

And I wanted Olia to be right. I wanted Dad to wait for us behind the bulwark, take us in the safety of the lifter and leave.

The sight of her climbing up the fence alone shook my thoughts away.

"What are you doing?" I yelled.

"I told you, Dad is on the opposite side!"

"You can't just go there, they'll shoot you!"

"No, they won't! Dad will tell them."

She sprang up on her feet and balanced on top of a barricade. Out of the cacophony of gunfire, a certain burst was strikingly distinct, as it brought Olia down with a yelp.

"Olia!" I heard myself cry.

Thirteen una-years and nine una-months ago

Now, this is a memory I seemed to have forgotten for a long time, perhaps because it has faded among many sleepless nights. Sleep was never easy for me, especially on this Planet. Thoughts about the encounter with you at first were hard to tackle, then the imagining of Penko persisted despite masturbating again and again. And even when I wasn't horny, this planet always offered something to think about, and if it wasn't the planet then it was my boyish body. Well, Phaethon and Eleczia's long days didn't help either.

Anyway, an una-hour had passed after going to bed when I heard Olia scream "no!" from her room. I knew you were with her. Soon after you arrived in our house, the bedtime story had turned into an everyday habit for Olia.

I must admit, at first, I thought if I let you kill her, I'd get rid of her...her Mom delusions, her annoying instrument playing, everything. Fortunately, the thought flew away as it came, and I threw my sheets away and got up.

I expected to crash upon Dad outside my door but he wasn't there. He was probably sleeping in his room. Could Mr. Stevens have sneaked in his bed? Damn, now this thought was even worse, and I hurried to open the door to Olia's room.

You were sitting by her side. She was upright, tears in her eyes. I expected her to lash at me for not knocking, but I think I saw relief calming her facial features at my sight.

"What's up?" I whispered as if I had interrupted some short of confession.

"Come," you said and showed me to Olia's bed, beside her.

"I don't want to hear about it," said Olia. "You are Mom and that's it."

"If you wish to call me 'Mom,' it is fine." I had heard you say the exact words as a reply to Olia's mom tantrums many times, and it never worked.

It didn't work now either.

"I'm not calling you 'Mom,' you are Mom!"

"Yes."

"No. You say it like you don't believe it." Now Olia looked angry, and I stopped in the middle of the room. I could predict the next words that came from her mouth. "I want both of you to leave."

You waited a second in hesitation. But when you got up, the move was robotically clumsy and blunt, and this must've aggravated Olia's mood.

"Get out!" she hissed. "Now! Both of you!"

You patted my back and ushered me outside.

You closed her door and looked at me. I eavesdropped to see if she was crying, but she wasn't. She was tough, Olia.

"I'll go back to her in a while. Don't worry."

"What was wrong?"

"I tried to tell her some things."

"Oh. Okay. Well..." I opened my door. "Goodnight. I guess?"

"Goodnight."

"But you were still standing outside my door when I got in."

"What?"

"Do you want to hear a story?" you said.

"Uhm..." I didn't, but I wouldn't be able to sleep either. "Sure. Come in."

I went to my bed, and you sat by my side. You had an almost imperceptibly musty smell which was soothing.

"Once upon a time," you started, using the ancient fairy tale triggering phrase, "there was a planet full of trees. The languages that were spoken were the languages of plants and its name was synonym to nature, to god, to planet, to everything. Then the Observers came. Creatures from another planet. They had two legs."

I thought then you were going to speak about humans, so I yawned, but you kept talking with your robotic voice that was even flatter than the voices of an automatic podcaster.

"And four hands," you added, and I was surprised. So, if this was the story of this planet, someone else had come before?

"They were peaceful creatures, fleeing a war-torn past. They took care not to trample the grass, not to hurt the trees, not to scare the animals. They didn't harm a single living thing. They had their own food, their own resources, their own technology. They didn't come to taste but to observe. They fell in love with this planet. And some of them decided to stay and change their name. From Observers to Gardeners."

Though the story had caught my interest, you started describing those aliens' daily life and however wonderful it might have seemed to you, it was boring to the ears of a teenager. Soon I felt my eyelids grow heavy.

"Those who left, did so in peace, without stealing a single seed. Those who stayed, did so to serve the Platani. They offered themselves as a gift. They put their existence in the strange armor they manufactured. And they transformed into something else."

You kept on going with more details, and I fell asleep before you finished your narration.

And this was probably the reason the remembrance of your visit ended up fading into something as faint as a past dream. Or perhaps it was because Olia later started telling her own version of this story, that the recollection of this night must've blended with her fairy tales.

It took time for this memory to surface. But when it did, it felt painfully true.

Thirteen una-years ago

It's you, isn't it?

You were faster to react. You grabbed Olia and crouched. I slammed on your shoulder and shook you both. You mopped a bit of blood from her forehead then put a palm on her heart.

Olia annoyed me, like all younger sisters do, but I couldn't afford to lose her. Not her too.

"Avra," you said. "Stay calm. It's a scratch. She's alive."

Blistering tears welled up in my eyes. I waited out the rain of bullets cracking into our barricades. I managed to get hold of myself, then I cupped my hands around my mouth and yelled, "Dad!"

Nothing happened. A shot glanced off a steel plate as if it was an answer to my scream.

I fished out my commbox, turned on the loudspeaker app and brought it to my mouth. I screamed for Dad. Again, and again, until, burst by burst, the shots ceased from the soldier's side.

You laid Olia down gently and stood up. For a moment nothing happened and my heart juddered—we were so close, we could be saved— then, a couple of bullets tinged at your frame, like nails pinned.

The shots came from the chlorobots' side. You stooped down, and I offered you the commbox—it was your turn. You refused with a nod, then you spoke. You didn't scream, but your voice boomed, as if you had turned up the volume.

"Neighbors. I'm Longest Roots. Don't shoot. These children. Are my seeds. Neighbors..."

Though I had heard the automata that barged into our house address you as Longest Roots, I didn't believe what Olia had told me, until the shots ceased from the chlorobots' side and I heard their prerecorded voices echo your name.

"Oh shit," I said, mostly to myself. "Olia was right, huh? You're all Platani... You did upload yourselves in the..."

With a decisive move you hurled Olia onto your shoulder, not sparing a glance at me. You slid over the barrier and turned to me, offering a wet metallic palm—rain, mud, leaking plasma, Olia's blood.

"Avra. It's true. Now move it."

I gave you my hand and you helped me onto the other side.

We walked hand in hand. You, limping like Penko. I struggled not to cry and failed. Straight ahead, behind the bulwark in the distance, I noticed a silhouette stand up, just like you did. I wiped soiled tears from my eyes that stung from the dirt. I rubbed them, and after a few more strides, I squinted and finally got to see.

It was Dad.

A burst from the chlorobots' side and he slumped down—was he shot or just taking cover? His body didn't flail; there was no blood splashing. The burst triggered an earsplitting fusillade of shots. I glanced back at the chlorobots' side. They had left their shelter and were charging onwards, the tips of their barrels flaring like sparkler candles. A couple of them sagged down as the soldiers shot back at them. The drone of the eight huge engines rose, hot gales kept thrashing on my face and the lifter levitated a bit higher. Its loading ramp was disconnected from its bay, gaping open in the air—it would soon be raised shut. And then we'd be left behind with all those furious chlorobots determined to kill us.

A grenade blasted a few meters forward, a gray umbrella slinging chunks of tarmac all over the apron. A piece slammed into my forehead.

"Now," you said, in a matter-of-fact way.

Then you yanked my arm violently and almost dislocated my shoulder as you ran for the bay.

Thirteen una-years and six una-months ago

"Oh, come on, Olia, I've had enough of your dreams..."

"But this was not a dream. Mom..."

"And cut this mom-crap, will you? Or I won't show you how to paint your nails."

Olia frowned. Though I had started painting my nails after you came into our house one and a half una-years ago, Olia had only asked me to teach her recently. If she didn't spend so much time with you, I'd have thought she was into someone.

"Who cares about nails anyway..." She puckered her lips in a grimace of restraining rage and her eyes glinted.

I yawned, lying on my bed. Lately, I was bored all the time except when in the presence of Penko. The gentle thrumming of rain on our roof was lulling me though it was just a long evening. The thunderstorm with the concrete cloud ceiling had probably given the meteorologists the opportunity for an unscheduled rain inside the skydome.

"Look," said Olia. "This was not a dream. Rocta told me everything in one of her bedtime stories. And it was supposed to be a secret."

I didn't fall for the secret trap. Whenever she came up with an outraging rumor, she told me it was a secret to make me feel guilty for my disbelief.

What you had just entrusted her with was supposedly the whole story of your past. The automata, you said, were a gift from another species that visited this planet long before humans named it Terra-Octa. These peaceful aliens, the Observers, never stole a single seed. Instead, some of them decided to stay and serve the Platani as their Gardeners. Before their comrades left, they put themselves in the armor they manufactured with the Platani's help. And they used to be bipeds but they transformed into something else after all those ages.

The story you had told me that night had already been tucked away in my mind and though Olia's fairy tale did remind me of something, I had grown so bored of her that I didn't make the connection.

She continued nonetheless.

Then the humans came. And when Dad started setting the woods on fire, the Platani connected through their roots and conferred. Some suggested to keep on fighting. Others wanted to wait and see how far humankind would go. A few preferred to quit life and let themselves wither into oblivion.

Their leader proposed surrender. She wanted to make peace with us, humans, learn from us and when the time was ripe, make us your allies. "Let only our past trunks die out," she said.

It was a hard choice, but the Platani decided as one. They uploaded their spirits into the Gardeners. The insides of their armor flourished and started radiating, a light so bright it flickered through their eyeholes.

Their leader was supposed to be you. The huge Platanus tree we had chanced upon on our first excursion.

Nice fairy tale, I thought. But I was bored. "So, who cares what the chlorobots were before and if the Platani uploaded themselves into them?"

"We do," replied Olia.

Thunder crackled—it should've hit the skydome close to our house. I yawned again. "Why?"

My commbox rang. Olia kept babbling—memories of those aliens, Avra, lingered in the Platani's minds, their long-forgotten wars, fighting skills, and—I stopped listening to her and read Penko's text. He had something important and "really, really classified" to show me. More secrets, then.

I heard Olia sigh as I texted back. I put my commbox back in my pocket. "So what?"

"They didn't surrender to become slaves. They never agreed to leave their armors and get into robotic frames—that was after their surrender!"

"You mean Dad forced them to..."

"I've no idea. What I do know is that we should free them. Unless we're up for a revolt."

I cackled. "A revolt? That's ridiculous. They surrendered while they were in their armor. How will they revolt now in those cheap-ass bot frames?"

"It's been two una-years since their surrender! Now they know everything about us! Our language, our defenses... Mom... Rocta said they've learned all about modern warfare from the best: us, humans. I think she told Dad, but he didn't..."

Our doorbell rang—so soon? Was Penko waiting outside in the rain?

"Okay, beat it, now. We'll talk another time."

"Wait... Should I speak to Dad?"

I heard Penko greet Mr. Stephens.

"No, we'll talk about it later. Now butt out, already!"

Olia frowned. The grave seriousness gave way to a mischievous smile. "All right, I'll butt out. Just don't make too much noise."

Penko stood by my doorway. My sister slipped out and I invited him in.

Olia sang, "Use a condom."

Penko's Adam's apple sprang up—it was as big as a nut and suddenly I was glad mine was tiny.

"Does she know?"

I gestured like I was shooing away a fly. "What is it?"

He glanced at the ajar door and plucked his commbox from his pocket, but it dropped from his hand. He picked it up. His moves were jerky, like the time we kissed—was he going to try again?

"What I'm about to sho-show you...is classified. Don't...don't ask me to send it to you, 'cause I won't, all right?"

"All right," I didn't recall him stuttering like that. Was he going to show me a recording of other kids making out?

He didn't. He sat on the floor with his back to the door and pointed the commbox's projection towards the wall, so he'd have the time to switch it off in case someone barged in.

The projection's resolution was so high it would be impossible to have been shot by a commbox or an implant camera. There was a table and a couple of chairs at the center of a dark, low-ceilinged chamber and five men—four fully strapped soldiers and a guy in a suit—standing in a semicircle around you.

You were crouched with your helmet lolled to your chest. Despite your position and the darkness, your armor still looked massive, your long arms stretching out. A coating of dust couldn't conceal either the green iridescence of your veins or the pulsing dots on your helmet's eye-slits.

Two soldiers kept a close watch, palms resting on their gun holsters, while the other two plucked away your pauldrons, your vambraces, your two-piece breastplate, your sabatons. Plate by plate they tossed them in a pile, revealing an anatomy of flywheels whirring in opaque blurs, turbine-like pumps spinning soundlessly, cogs, cylinders and accumulators—a golden hydraulic system of Lilliputian parts detailed to perfection. A web of radiant arteries corded throughout your frame and when the soldiers stripped you off your helmet, I was shocked to see a throbbing, radiant, jelly green mass resting on the grail-like cup on top of your gorget. The soldiers cringed away, and Penko's palm cupped mine—it was hot and sweaty. Could Olia's fairy tale have any truth in it? Could this slimy lump be what that alien race turned into after years of serving you?

True or false, this slimy lump was definitely you.

"Go on."

I jolted. This was Dad's voice; and I couldn't help but check the room as if he had sneaked in. But no, his voice came from the recording. I guessed he was standing next to someone shooting the scene since Dad wouldn't bother recording it himself.

The soldiers put four trembling hands on the mass. They caught it and started to pull slowly and carefully. The veins strained like taut tentacles but wouldn't give in. Meanwhile, another guard tried a pauldron on his shoulder. Despite the whole armor being much larger, it seemed to fit. Perhaps it was because the automata's armor had long limbs rather than torso.

Dad let out a sharp cough and the guard threw the pauldron back on the pile—*clank*.

The soldiers started wrenching you left and right and with a series of plops and small bursts of plasma splashing all over the various moving parts, the tentacles got ripped and unfolded around bone-like rods. They slid out, their shredded capillaries bleeding plasma. The flywheels slowed down, the cogs decelerated, the pumps ceased spinning. Every little part inside your armor came to a halt.

The man in the suit was gawking at you with carnivorous astonishment. His face was familiar—oh, yeah, I'd seen him in the local newsfeed.

"Wait, isn't this guy...?"

"Yes." Penko told me his name. "The Pacifist congressman."

"Isn't he supposed to oppose Dad?"

"Well, that's what he openly says..."

"But..."

"Shh, we'll talk about it later."

The soldiers managed to pluck you out of your frame. They placed you on the table and you looked like a bleeding octopus. Flesh strings branching out to the floor, swaying as they shrank back slowly like a snail pulling in its shell. A pool of dark plasma spread on the aluminum surface, flowed to the table's edge and started dripping.

The congressman came close and bent to examine you. A drop of plasma splashed on his leather shoe, and he pulled back in disgust.

I was perplexed. The more I stared at you, the more the bulges and crinkles on your lump seemed symmetrical. Their shapes were shifting in a combined way, rippling in fluidic synchronicity like yolks on a broken egg. They never mingled into each other, always maintaining a vague integrity. And did they form something like a blurry face? There, left and right, were two large spherical humps that could've been eyes and amidst them and a tad lower two tiny holes—nostrils?—and below these holes, a small slit that could've been a mouth, and—look—a tumor slipping in and out of it, like a tongue.

The soldiers that stripped you disappeared from view and came back tugging an old robotic frame. They left it helmetless in a crouched position—it was the body I've known you as ever since you came to our house. Compared to your previous armor it looked small and insignificant. Poor. Then, the soldiers went by the table.

"No, not you two," said Dad and the pairs switched. I've no idea why he did it; perhaps to remind them who was in charge. Anyway, the two guards exchanged a glance and the one that tried your pauldron on rubbed his nose. They almost had a fight trying to coordinate. They sorted it out and carried you, your shredded tentacles oozing out on the floor. Then they placed you on the frame's collar, where the robot's AI processor used to be housed.

"Is it that simple?" said the congressman.

"No," replied Dad, a bit bluntly. "The engineers modified the frames. Thing is, these modifications were easy and cheap. And low maintenance too. No batteries, no recharging... They feed on plants."

"And... And they agreed to this? I mean, they did surrender but..."

Dad didn't answer.

"You didn't give them a choice, did you?"

"Their leader consented to this. You'll see," said Dad.

Penko put the recording in fast forward as your tentacles branched out again, slipping inside the frame. He paused when the soldiers put on your helmet. Two green lanterns lit up through the eye-slits of the white, plastic humanoid façade with the silicon details.

Dad came close to you.

"Do you understand me?"

You stood still for a while. Then, you jolted, a whirring noise kicked off and your body shook violently. Everyone stepped back until the shaking dwindled.

You raised your head and looked at him. You nodded.

"Good. Can you move your hand?"

You lifted an arm, clenched your fist, unclenched, stretched your fingers. The moves were sloppier than you'd expect from a bot, but I guess this was your first time in this body, cause you had gotten a hold of it when I met you.

"Get up."

You obeyed clumsily and despite the comicality of your movement, a soldier unholstered his gun.

"Are you satisfied in this frame?" horned in the congressman.

A few seconds passed. A few seconds where I could hear my own heartbeat, or perhaps it was Penko's or the heartbeats of the people in the recording.

You nodded.

"Damn," mumbled the congressman.

"Good," said Dad. "The talking module will take a bit more time. If your people prove cooperative, we'll provide you with more advanced frames."

"That's one wicked idea, General," said the congressman.

"And I'll need your support on this."

The congressman grinned. "We'll need to talk this out in detail, later, but I'll definitely review the findings of my inspection. Now... Shall we?"

And now that I thought about it, this guy's resistance to Dad's plans was rather lukewarm. He had remained silent for a long time, hadn't he?

In the recording, he left with Dad. Before the door clanged shut and the recording tumbled to a stop, his voice was heard, "But I have to congratulate you, General. We might have just found the most suitable workforce for this planet's atmosphere."

The projection disappeared.

I felt as if I was teleported back to my room, beside Penko.

"You think I should show it to Olia?" he asked after a while.

"No... No way..."

"Then, I...I will delete this, all right?"

I agreed. Dad claimed publicly that the chlorobots consented to switch bodies but this footage suggested otherwise. And if the footage fell into the wrong hands, other Pacifists could...

"Girls?" Dad's voice made us both jump up. It wasn't a glitch in Penko's commbox app. He was standing right behind the door, outside my room. We exchanged a glance of horror. Could he have seen us? No, the door was closed, unless he had taken a peak inside and then shut it back silently...

Shit, I was making things up. I got up and opened the door, my knees shaking. He had moved and was now by Olia's door, dressed in camo coveralls. He smiled when he saw us. "Hey there. You know where Olia is?"

It was strange to hear him after the recording. It was as if he was a different person. Yet his voice was always different when he wasn't among his troops.

"Urm... I guess she finished studying and..." I hadn't noticed when the unscheduled rain had ceased. "Perhaps she went outside?"

Dad frowned. "All right. Something's wrong? You both look like you've seen a ghost..."

Dad could smell trouble, and I'd have let a torrent of questions sluice out of my mouth if it wasn't for Penko that replied, "No, General Brahms, nothing's wrong."

"Okay, then let's go downstairs. I've got something to tell you."

"Uhm... I was... I was just about to leave," said Penko and I walked him out the front door.

"You're leaving me alone, *now*?" I hissed before he left.

"Don't panic. He knows nothing."

"Avra," Dad's voice. "Come on."

I shut the door. Dad gestured at me towards the backyard, and I noticed his implant flashing in his eye. He was talking to someone. "I'll be right there in a second," he whispered.

I dragged my feet to the backyard.

Lightning coupled the inky cotton ceiling of the skydome in a flash of luminous roots that coated its curvature. The scheduled rain had ended and the lamps in the garden made the damp grass sparkle. You and Olia were tending that small, scraggly Platanus tree Dad had planted—eventually, it would outgrow our backyard and uproot our house, but it'd take hundreds of years.

And it didn't look as if it was ever going to happen.

"Why does it have no veins?" asked Olia. "Is it because it's a baby?"

I'd horn in and tell her to ask it in her sleep but she'd quit that fable since you came in, two una-years ago. Truth is, she'd quit all of her naïve fantasies and was only interested in gardening.

"Yes," you replied. "And no. Its veins should've been larger. And its color should've been..."

You let your sentence trail off and turned around towards us, as if our presence was the reason that you didn't finish your explanation.

"Avra," said Mr. Stephens behind me, "did Penko leave already?"

"Yes." I approached the Platanus tree and stood next to Olia. You were pruning twigs here and there.

Olia sighed. "Well, it's not that it has no veins at all... It's just that they seem...hollow..."

She was right. The tree's arteries had thinned and adhered to its bark like withered ivy.

I touched the bark. "It's not hot either," I said.

Olia frowned. "It's like it's dead." Lightning turned the evening into day. Thunder crashed simultaneously—it must've hit the skydome again.

"Why should its bark be hot?" asked Mr. Stephens.

I sighed. Hadn't he ever touched a tree in the jungle? Excursions weren't common due to the equipment, but still.

"Well, *all* Platani veins are hot. If you'd touched one, you'd know that," said Olia.

His brows furrowed. "Actually, during our last walk with your dad it didn't seem so hot."

Oh, so he had been on an excursion. I don't know how he'd managed to talk Dad into renting suits and helmets and going out together but obviously he did.

Clack—you clipped a branch. I fantasized about snatching that pruner from your hands and stabbing his trunk of a leg with it. His presence, his relationship with Dad that seemed to get closer and more intimate by every passing day, the fact that he'd prod us daily with the things they did together. I wanted him away from our house. I wanted to tell Dad that we didn't need to have someone replace Mom. Well, I didn't. And Olia too, since she looked just fine spending time with you.

But I never told him anything. It's like I never had the chance to, since Dad, contrary to Mr. Stephens, never mentioned him unless necessary.

"I guess it has something to do with what *Mom* told me," replied Olia. "Right, Mom?"

What were we talking about? Oh, about the tree's temperature and how its veins seemed hollow. And she probably meant that the reason was that the Platani trees had uploaded themselves into the automata.

Dad spoke, saving Mr. Stephens from falling into the she-is-not-your-mom trap.

"Hey, girls!"

"Hey, Dad!" said Olia. I still felt numb from the recording I'd watched. Mr. Stephens didn't share my hesitation. He hopped over to Dad and hugged him. So, their relationship *had* escalated.

Dad gently nudged him away.

Olia and I shared a glance.

"Okay, gather up," said Dad. "I've got news for you."

"What news, Dad?" asked Olia.

"Well…" His Adam's apple sprang up. "We're leaving this place!"

Thirteen una-years ago

It's you, isn't it?

We were slow and our last run felt even slower in the clamor of thunder, gunfire, explosions, screams and the engines' drone growing louder at every sapping step. Still, I could hear your joints creaking, your spinning parts fluttering, your limbs clunking. How much time before you collapsed? How much time before the unfiltered air made us sick? Olia was hanging limp on your shoulder, bouncing like a half-filled sack—wait, did she open her eyes? Yes, she did, she looked around in horror, then she noticed me and held on to you tight.

The temperature spiked up as we got past the soldier's bulwark, and I couldn't help but steal a glance—was Dad one of the corpses lying on his comrades' boots? I couldn't see and I wouldn't release your hand and be left behind. My eyes hurt, boiling in the eight turbines' scorching heat blasting from above us. The area covered by the umbrella of the lifter's legs had turned into a furnace of turbulent air. The deafening drone had numbed my hearing too and I tried to catch my breath, but you dragged me up the steel steps to the bay's platform.

The lifter was hovering above us, its loading ramp slowly rising a few meters away. In a few seconds it would shut and the lifter would launch to the sky, to the starship in orbit.

The flow of desperate humans trying to escape was thicker as we approached, like a cataract spewing from the ramp in reverse. Just like us, they had reached the last step to safety, just like they knew it was their last chance.

A group of soldiers stood on the ramp's lip helping up whomever came close, urging the rest to hurry up. A team of whitecoats—scientists I guessed—formed a chain and were loading up huge sacks in a corner—a bundle of soiled roots protruded from one, I guess it was Platani. Though the lifter's bulk above us protected us from the rain, the engine's hot gales thrashed my hair on my burning eyes. Up on the lifter's loading ramp was a stooped soldier, a woman with a shaved head. She helped up a grannie, pushed her in and then got on her feet. She nudged a giant of a man beside her who had just heaved up a kid—maybe the grannie's grandchild. She pointed at us, and they both stopped and stared. At you.

You sped up, your clutch crushing my palm. Though I couldn't hear my own voice in the earsplitting drone, I yelled and waved with my other hand to the soldiers.

The giant ushered the kid in the darkness of the lifter's hull but the woman took out her gun and aimed.

You didn't flinch, just kept hobbling onwards, pulling me along, pushing against bodies—and I can only guess that it was because of those people around us that the woman didn't dare to shoot at you.

Yet.

With every inch that we came closer to safety, we were offering her a clearer shot.

But then, the giant patted her shoulder and with cupped hands around his mouth, spoke in her ear. I blinked and in a flash of clarity I recognized Mr. Stephens—how had he managed to get here before us?

The woman lowered her gun. Mr. Stephens started waving and screaming mutely, his lips forming our names.

Despite the cacophony of noises, a wave of screams rose around us.

The ramp started folding up slowly. Bodies crushed against you, threatening to throw us, and you thrust what was left of your robotic armor back at them. Though it was barely functioning, its mass hadn't changed and it was heavy, so you managed to soldier on.

But when we finally got to the ramp, it was too high. Some people were hanging mid-air from its lip.

Someone tried to grab your hand; you elbowed his face and threw him away. This was kill or be killed, and if it wasn't for you, neither I nor Olia would've made it even up to here.

The ramp rose a few inches more.

You brought Olia forward, caught her by the hips—she tried to hug you. You shook her hard, violently, as if you wanted to hurt her, and for a moment I was scared that you had changed sides, but when she loosened her grip, you jumped and flung her up.

Two pliers of hands grasped her by the armpits. Mr. Stephens lifted her up the ramp that was gaining more height. Then he lay down again and reached out for me. He was screaming my name, though I couldn't make out his voice.

I thought it was over for me and you, but the feeling of relief that Olia had made it wouldn't let despair take hold over me.

But nothing was over yet.

With a clumsy yet decisive move, you seized me and hurled me on your shoulder. Even like this, the ramp was too high, and you didn't lift me up. Had you lost your strength, finally? No, because you sidled and I noticed an army vehicle that had cropped up beside you somehow. A soldier stood on its hood and a couple of his comrades—one was the woman with the shaved head—were pulling him up. Other people took notice of it as if it had cropped up right now. You clambered on its hood, first out of all the people around you, with a speed that I didn't know your body was capable of. Perhaps its speed limitations had ceased working? I do not know. The soldiers on the ramp saw you but Mr. Stephens was already there, nudging them away. He lay down so he could give me his hand.

You stood on the vehicle's hood and lifted me by the waist. I raised my head. Mr. Stephens' stretched out trunk arms were getting higher and further away from us.

His lips moved, "Avra!"

By now, I had full confidence in your determination. I knew that if I wouldn't make it to the ramp, you'd end up grabbing a turbine and pulling the whole lifter down to save me.

You jumped and flung me in the air. Low gravity helped and at the last moment I snatched Mr. Stephens' palm, and as he pulled me up, I felt as if he'd pluck my arm out of my shoulder.

He left me on the ramp. Olia was with us too.

"Get Mom too!" screamed Olia—the ramp was folding up and I could barely hear her.

On the ground, people swarmed around the vehicle.

"Where's your mom?" The bald woman searched among the people hanging from the ramp.

"There!" Mr. Stephens pointed at you, but didn't lie down again.

"The fucking chloropunk?"

The gap was getting smaller, the ramp was about to shut, and we were already too high to get you too. Two other soldiers were pulling on a rope from which a man was hanging, spinning around as it wound and unwound like a pendulum.

"Help her!" screamed Olia at Mr. Stephens. She tried to punch his wall of a belly, but she could barely raise her fists. The man hanging from the rope lost his grip and plummeted to the ground, falling on the raised hands of people who were crying.

"Fuck my life," said Mr. Stephens and darted in the soldiers' direction. They fell back, letting go of the rope, but Mr. Stephens snatched it. He lay on the ramp's lip, and tossed the rope to you.

It hit your face; you could have just reached for it, grabbed it and let Mr. Stephens carry you to safety.

But you didn't move an inch. You just stood there, on top of the vehicle's hood, a buzzing, desperate crowd around you, staring at us as we were leaving. The lifter took a couple of meters with a jolt and Mr. Stephens almost tumbled out. I tried to grab him—a stupid idea, he was too heavy. Luckily, he got up.

Olia stood frozen, staring at the rope falling down. Her gaze landed on you. You raised your hand and waved goodbye. I imagined a smile painted on your plastic façade. As the lifter gained height, I felt my heart lighten up, then sneezed. I was still cold and wet and exhausted, yet we were saved, at least Olia and I. I even dared to hope I'd been mistaken before and Dad wasn't the man I'd seen fall down on the bulwark. He could be inside the lifter—though I knew deep inside that he'd be the last to leave. And later on, maybe I'd see Penko's face smiling at us, as if his death was another prank of his.

At his memory, I suddenly felt myself empty of emotions and alone. It was me and Olia. Dad, Penko, you, everyone else was staying back.

I turned to Olia—the need to hug her overwhelming me—but her expression was blank. I didn't dare to move.

Something felt terribly wrong. The eight engines boomed, the lifter soared up, my stomach tightened from the sudden acceleration before the ramp shut. With all the strength that was left inside me, I reached out for her.

But I was too late. Olia flung herself out of the ramp.

Thirteen una-years and six una-months ago

"Wait...is everyone leaving?" asked Olia.

"No," replied Dad. "Just us. I mean, some other..."

"Then, no!" cried Olia and scurried to stand in front of him, as if to block his way to the garden. "No, Dad, no... I mean...if others are staying, why can't we stay here too?"

He raised an eyebrow, which usually was a controlled gesture to show interest, but now it was obvious that my sister had caught him by surprise. He must've thought we didn't like New Istanbul's confined environment, the learning modules, Mr. Stephens' robotic smile—was that oaf happy to get back to Terra-Dua?

"Wha... What happened, dear?" he asked Dad. Since that stroll they took in the jungle he'd dropped "General Brahms." At least they had to wear suits and helmets they couldn't take off. But now, "dear," "honey," and "love" were all used daily. As if having him around wasn't annoying enough.

Dad glanced at him, not the slightest bit of annoyance showing in his face. "This is confidential, but, well, you're part of the family now."

I wanted to scream, "What?" But curiosity won over my anger.

"The initial estimates have proved inaccurate," said Dad. "The quantities of Chloron yielded by the Platani and the rest of the trees are less than anticipated and they keep dropping. If the situation goes on like this, Chloron won't be profitable to harvest for long."

Did you freeze for a moment?

Olia's eyes bulged out. I thought that she'd keep nagging but she said, "I told you that the Platani are hollow now! That's why their veins are withered! Without their sentience they're dying!"

"Well, I don't think they're dying, honey," said Dad. "But, yes, the scientists have noticed various transformations... One of them being their withered veins."

"I guess another one is their temperature," I stared spitefully at Mr. Stephens. "They're not hot anymore, are they?"

Mr. Stephens ignored me. "So, we're abandoning the colony, honey?"

Dad went to the table and touched the chair—it was wet. He leaned on the table's edge. Mr. Stephens followed him and perched next to him. Though you started pruning the sick Platanus tree again, I had the impression your attention was fixed on our conversation.

But how could the face of a robot indicate that it's eavesdropping? Well, maybe I was just imagining things, right?

"Hell no," said Dad. "The colony stays where it's put. Terra-Octa has plenty of other resources to harvest. It's just that..."

Clack, the pruner's blades.

Dad sighed as if the sound had interrupted his train of thoughts.

"Then... Why are we leaving?" asked Mr. Stephens.

"Well, with the Pacifists' party rising in popularity and the upcoming elections... I mean the planet's shares have plunged already, so my superiors decided a General of my caliber is not justified here anymore. They'll get someone else for sure to make do, of course."

He eyed each one of us, except you.

"As for you"—he raised his hand and rubbed Mr. Stephens' thick neck—"you can stay or you can come back in Terra-Dua. Whatever suits you."

I think I heard Mr. Stephens purr as he closed his eyes.

Present

It's you, isn't it?

This eerie whistle of your flywheels is so much quieter than the whirring of the crude, human-made hydraulics of the robotic frame they'd put you in. And gone is the jade scintillation of your eyes that studded the plastic façade you had. Your helmet's eyeholes are dark.

Your limbs flute as you approach, firing up a rustle of nervousness that rises behind me. Please excuse my colleague's disquiet; it's the first time they face your kind and, may I remind you, you're a sight to behold. A golden giant, a gait so fluid it's as if there are no cogs inside your armor—nothing like that frail clunker of a body that squeaked noisily in your last run to save me and my sister.

And, to be honest, the reason I've come here is her.

Thirteen una-years ago

After Olia leaped out of the lifter, I fell on the ramp's skirt and craned my head below, only to catch a glimpse of the ground plummeting down. But before I had the chance to spot where Olia had landed, Mr. Stephens shoved me back in and the ramp finally folded up shut.

The distance to the ground had seemed enormous, but we were already climbing up high, fast. So, her fall must've been survivable. At least, that's what I convinced myself with time.

The soldiers strapped me in a spare seat along with other children—the lifter was brimmed, and adults had to sit on the cargo compartment's floor. The whole place was shaking and rattling as it soared up.

"The machine is overweight," said Penko beside me. "It's going to break apart."

"No, it's not, you fool," I snapped.

A rush of changing emotions swept over me: surprise (Penko in here?); turned to joy (he's alive!); turned to realization as I blinked twice (he's not Penko, he doesn't even look like him); turned to despair (Penko, Dad and Olia are all gone).

Inside the starship, children were the first to be tended against the diseases and infections of Terra-Octa's atmosphere. Medicine was scarce and a lot of people perished the following days. Some soldiers told me they'd seen Dad. He had stood his ground during the chlorobots' final charge. None had seen him getting shot down though.

For years I used to dream that you lived and convinced the chlorobots to spare the people who got left behind. And if the prospect of Dad surrendering seemed farfetched even in a delusion, I did allow myself to hope that perhaps Olia might have somehow made it.

Present

But now, at the sight of your brilliant army—equipped with those strange golden rifles that look as if they've been made from the same metal used to forge your armor—I see the truth.

You left no one alive, did you? No adults, no children. I blame you not. Did you bury her?

You don't need to answer. I understand.

I guess you'd like to know the reason we've returned after all this time.

You'd assume that following your revolt, humankind would send a force to devastate your entire planet. But upon our arrival to Terra-Dua, we discovered the Pacifists had come to power. They had promised to develop interplanetary ethics, establish procedures for terraforming and exploration of possible Terras, respecting the local life. We shouldn't just rush and exploit every new planet, they said. We hadn't turned our back on internal colonialism to start all over again on an interplanetary scale, right?

Then again, perhaps you were lucky because other materials replaced Chloron. It could be that we humans were lucky too, not having to take you on.

As righteous as the Pacifists' intentions might be, the proposed changes didn't happen overnight. We had to endure lots of turmoil, changes and reforms. But the will of the people was steadfast. Terra-Octa's example should be the last.

I've gone through all this in my university studies on Interplanetary Affairs.

Though the Terra-Octa's attempt of colonization was to be labeled as a failure, Dad was named a hero. I know now the courage Mr. Stephens glorified in his funeral speech was pure foolhardiness. His legacy was his contacts and, I must admit, Mr. Stephens. My past caretaker honored the vow they had exchanged a few days before the riot, although they never got a chance to marry officially. Without his support for all those years, I would have never managed to become an interplanetary ambassador and lead this mission.

So, I represent humankind in its entirety when I say I'm here to offer you our sincerest apologies. And to let you know we've changed.

We want to establish a new relationship with your kind. And to start with, we'd like to trade with you. We can offer technology, information, knowledge. And maybe, when we gain your trust, we could rent some land on this beautiful planet of yours, in your terms and conditions and with full respect of its tenants.

I don't know if you can speak in this form, Rocta, but I know you understand my language and can write, even on this fertile soil. And now that you tower over me, I'm certain you're still the leader of your kin. Take as long as you need to think our offer over. I can wait, or I can leave and return, or leave forever, should you request so.

And allow me to ask you one more time. After you announce your decision, please tell me what happened to my sister.

Thirteen una-years and four una-months ago

Since Dad announced that we're leaving, Olia frittered away all of her time with you. She even went on to blab to Dad all about your story, but he didn't seem to care. This planet was none of his business anymore.

So, Penko and I had a few chances to be alone and that evening we visited New Istanbul's ramparts. They looked deserted. Following your surrender, Dad had gradually decreased the number of guards. It wasn't the first time I was sitting here gazing at the plains the forestry mulchers had flattened out, pushing the jungle's fringes out of sight. But this time, everything seemed to share a darker tint. The distant drone of copters, the buzzing of the city's vehicles, even the chomp of Penko's jaws as he munched those favorite gums of his seemed to carry the unease of waiting out a funeral of someone you barely knew.

He placed his hand on mine. "It's only a few una-years till college. And perhaps my family will decide to leave this place too after a while..."

A knot in my throat choked my reply. His hand crawled up my arm until his arm wrapped around my shoulder. I leaned against his chest.

He pulled me closer, and I breathed in a waft of alien mint. "I won't forget you, Avra."

I stifled a sob. We had mocked plenty of melodramatic farewells in movie scenes. The memory pinched me. Were we going to watch a movie together again?

He fished out a package of gum. "Why don't you try one of these?"

"Well, you never offered one."

He laughed dryly. I took one.

Time passed by and the mint taste dwindled in my mouth. The evening was dying at Eleczia's slow descent. Time wipes out everything in the end. Minutes to dry your tears, hours to swallow your sobs, days or, perhaps, months to numb your sadness. How much time to bring back happiness?

"I wanted to talk to you about something else," said Penko.

I accidentally gulped down the gum—it burned my throat. I rubbed my eyes and pulled away from his hug. During the last una-year he had lost weight, gotten taller and a few acne pimples had grown on his fuzzy cheeks. I was tall too, but the blockers had stopped most of my boyish body's nuisances. I thought that he was going to talk about us.

"I think I've done something stupid..."

"What?" My voice wasn't as hoarse as his.

"Remember that classified holo I showed you?"

"The one with Rocta..."

"No, not that one, the other one. The first one. The one recorded in the congress."

"Yeah, that's old, isn't it?"

"It is. I sent it to a friend of mine... And I think he sent it to another..."

"So what?"

"So... I think it leaked and now many chloropunks have seen it and they're angry and I might get in trouble..."

"What's up, you believe Olia's tales now?"

"No, but..."

I sighed. "When did you do this?"

"It's been a while... Before your dad announced that we're leaving."

For some reason, I remembered the way it seemed to me as if you were eavesdropping while Dad was telling us about our departure. As if what he was saying was changing your plans.

What plans? I shooed the thought away from my mind. I was just numb at the prospect of losing Penko.

"The chlorobots are peaceful. What kind of trouble can a stupid holo cause?"

Present

The moment stretches in utter stillness as if everyone is frozen. You, towering over me, your army of golden automata lined up behind you, my colleagues behind me.

Then, with a melodic whistle, you move. You put your strange, golden rifle on the ground like you did so long ago in front of New Istanbul's walls. I open my mouth to tell you that this must be a misunderstanding, your surrender is not what we came here for—but you don't kneel, you just bend down slightly and bring your hands to your helmet. You turn it—left, click, right, click—it unlatches and you ease it off.

I falter back and lean into the arms of some of my colleagues—I've no idea who they are, but if they didn't catch me, I'd have tumbled down as if I'd been punched in the face.

Could I be dreaming? My eyes douse in an opaque pool, the fiery prelude of a fountain of tears. And no matter how many times I blink, what my eyes see cannot be erased.

It wasn't just you that took the helmet off. All the automata left their rifles to follow suit. Now I see why there was no emerald scintillation inside your eyeholes, inside all the automata's eyeholes. Because there's no alien lump inside, puppeteering your frame. You're not Rocta. And your army are not automata.

Heads jut out through the gorgets of a thousand gleaming armors. Their skin has a pale chartreuse tint like the chewing gum Penko used to eat, yet they're unmistakably human.

Some are young, some are old. Most of them are strangers, a few look familiar, and maybe a couple of them ring a bell. Yet the face towering above me, I know all too well. In spite of the riper features and its mint complexion, there's no chance I'm wrong.

It's you, Olia, my sister. Isn't it?

* * *

Yes, Avra, it's me, Olia, and I'm glad to see your eyes in a face that suits you. I remember how much you craved this. And this army of automata behind me are not the ones that revolted that day. They're what has become of the humans you left behind. You should call us Gardeners.

I apologize for this surprise, Avra, but I'm not Mom—you don't mind me calling her "Mom," now, do you? Oh, I got rid of all my childish delusions long ago, don't you worry. I know I'm not the Chosen One. I was just too damn lucky to chance upon Mom.

Now, let me fill in the missing pieces of her story for you.

She was still alive when I crashed down from the lifter. My legs were shattered, and my spine broken. Yes, the machine had already soared high to the sky when I fell, and I was lucky I made it. She took me in her arms and bent over me to keep me safe from the ongoing fight.

The soldiers defending the bulwark fought till the last man standing. Dad was among them. I guess he died as he had dreamt of. But, between you and me, I guess he died like a fool.

The rest gave up. The automata—I'll keep calling them automata though, as I told you before you left this planet, they were the Platani—herded all the humans in the devastated apron to decide upon their fate.

Some, of course, suggested to kill them.

But Mom stuck to her beliefs. She suggested giving us a chance to repent. We could become their Gardeners, demolish the city, plant new trees, help bring back the balance.

The Platani, fully integrated with the alien creatures they had uploaded themselves into, left their robotic frames and planted themselves back in the soil to sprout new trees. So, they let us take the armor from the museum where they'd been kept—Dad's one decision that was definitely right. That's all we needed to survive in this planet's atmosphere and serve the trees.

I took Mom's armor.

Of course, we didn't have a choice. But we did take pride in our new task. We did find purpose. Allow me to say, maybe more than any other human has.

Mom didn't make it. She had spent all her plasma that day. And she never asked for help, not until everything important was decided.

This is Mom's story, Sister. And now, please let me relay the Platani's wishes to you, as their humble servant.

You say you represent humankind. And you're here to offer your apologies. You claim you've changed.

Yet here you are calling me Rocta—not Longest Roots. You call this planet Terra-Octa. Did you ever ask the name the Platani gave it?

You say you want to establish a new relationship with them. But the Platani are no rulers here. They're merely servants of the soil, of the planet. Of nature.

Dad was right. War is a pest that humans lug with them. Even if they don't get to start it, it gets to bug its way into everything they touch. And we don't need that. We don't need your trade, your technology, your information, your knowledge. If humans want to rebuild their Terras, if they want ecological energy, they need to find their own ways.

All humankind had to offer was us, the Gardeners.

You want to gain the Platani's trust? Let *us* do our job, tend to the trees. If you want to respect this planet's tenants, show respect in their way, not yours.

Stay away.

Oh, and before you leave, I've got a gift for you, Sister. It's nothing of importance, but I do remember grownups saying the memory enhancement modules make it harder to forget lost loves. Anyway, let me open this box for you. I apologize, but this was the best place I had to preserve it. Here you are. I took it from his pocket before we buried him.

* * *

Time has turned the paper's color into white and erased the Platanus tree sketch. Yet it's easy to recognize that the gift that Olia gives me is a package of Penko's chewing gum.

ABOUT THE AUTHOR

Antony Paschos is a Greek author with short stories in *Interzone, Galaxy's Edge, ZNB Presents, Giganotosaurus, James Gunn's Ad Astra*, and other magazines. He has published four books in Greek and one in French. His work has been translated into four more languages. He is a member of the Athens Club of Science Fiction, and lives in Athens.

Please take a moment to review this book at your favorite retailer's website, Goodreads, or simply tell your friends!

www.ingramcontent.com/pod-product-compliance
Lightning Source LLC
Chambersburg PA
CBHW020732310726
48969CB00003B/799